Jane Austen

PRIDE AND PREJUDICE

Notes by Geoffrey Nash

BA (OXFORD) PH D (LONDON)
formerly Lecturer in English Literature,
Omdurman University, Sudan

YORK PRESS
Immeuble Esseily, Place Riad Solh, Beirut.

ADDISON WESLEY LONGMAN LIMITED
Edinburgh Gate, Harlow,
Essex CM20 2JE, England
Associated companies, branches and representatives
throughout the world

First published 1980
Twentieth impression 1997

ISBN 0-582-02297-5

Produced by Longman Singapore Publishers Pte Ltd
Printed in Singapore

Contents

Part 1

Introduction

Jane Austen's life

Jane Austen was born in 1775. Her father was a clergyman in the Hampshire village of Steventon and she was the last but one of a family of eight children. Jane and her sister Cassandra, her senior by two years, were the only girls. The brothers adopted such professions as were open to their social class: the eldest, James, was for a time a scholar at Oxford before becoming a cleric, while Jane's favourite, Henry, was at one time a banker, before he too entered orders. Francis and Charles were in the Navy. Of the five professions generally said to be open to men of rank — politics, the Church, law, medicine, and the armed services — the Austens seemed to have a marked preference for the Church and the Navy. Jane was to include a number of characters from those professions in her books. Yet another of her brothers, Edward, was adopted by a member of the landed gentry, and became a country gentleman. So Jane Austen had ample models in real life for the characters we meet in her books.

Jane herself lived a quiet life. She attended several schools until the end of her formal education, when she was only eleven. Like Elizabeth Bennet, she had around her the means to educate herself if she wished. Her father was a fine scholar with a good library, but the Austens did not try to hide the fact that they read novels. This is perhaps surprising, for, as Jane Austen wrote in *Northanger Abbey*, novel-reading was still something to which only young ladies would readily admit. Jane acquired a thorough knowledge of English eighteenth-century literature, including the moral philosophy of Dr Johnson (1709–84), the poetry of William Cowper (1731–1800), as well as the novelist's technique of Samuel Richardson (1689–1761) and Henry Fielding (1707–54). In addition, she was much influenced by Fanny Burney (1752–1840), a novelist and contemporary of hers, who wrote about the same kind of society as she, in such works as *Evelina* (1778) and *Camilla* (1796).

Jane was soon busily writing. As a teenager, her writings already showed an original wit and liveliness. But this was apparently not an outstanding thing in her family, for all of them were accounted to be very talented.

Jane attended balls with her sister in Basingstoke and was quite familiar with fashionable society from an early age. Though she wrote so much about marriage, she herself was destined not to marry. She and her sister Cassandra both had suitors, and both appear to have lost serious lovers in tragic circumstances. Certainly, Cassandra's fiancé, a chaplain in the Navy, was drowned at sea, and it seems likely that Jane's only serious love also died before there was even an engagement. So the sisters remained at home with their mother, and the only other events in their lives were several changes of house, all in an area of about a hundred miles. The last years were spent in the village of Chawton in Hampshire, where Jane doted on her many nephews and nieces. Apart from writing frequent letters to her family and friends, Jane was now occupied mainly with her novels, until she suddenly became ailing in 1816. She died the next year in a house near Winchester Cathedral where she had been moved in the hope of a cure. Thus, befittingly, the English novelist, who in many ways was a product of the eighteenth century but who lived into the Romantic era, was buried within sight of the orderly Georgian architecture of the Cathedral close. On her stone is inscribed:

> The benevolence of her heart, the sweetness of her temper, and the extraordinary endowment of her mind obtained the regard of all who knew her, and the warmest love of her intimate connections.

The novels

Jane Austen's novels were published between 1811 and 1817, but three, *Sense and Sensibility*, *Pride and Prejudice*, and *Northanger Abbey*, were begun when she was a young woman. Both *Sense and Sensibility* and *Pride and Prejudice* were at first written as letters from one character to another (the 'epistolary style', which was common in the eighteenth century). Although one or more of these early works were sent to a publisher, Jane's work did not appear in print until the early novel, Elinor and Marianne, was rewritten and appeared as *Sense and Sensibility* in 1811. Then came *Pride and Prejudice* (1813); *Mansfield Park* (1814); *Emma* (1816); and *Northanger Abbey* and *Persuasion* together in 1817.

The general background

England was undergoing rapid change in Jane Austen's lifetime. The economy was changing from an agricultural to an industrial one. In 1815, the population of Great Britain was thirteen million and still growing. From the time of Jane's maturity the continent of Europe was involved in war. At times, Britain was isolated from the whole of Europe which was controlled by Napoleon. This caused much distress amongst the poor who saw the price of corn rise steadily. Revolutionary ideas were gaining ground in opposition to the aristocratic world of the eighteenth century. At the same time a Christian revival was taking place. John Wesley (1703–91) had founded Methodism, a message of urgent spiritual salvation to the ordinary people. Times were indeed changing.

Yet Jane Austen's novels hardly mirror all this. *Pride and Prejudice* mentions 'the restoration of peace' in the final chapter, a reference to one of the short intervals in the European war. But otherwise we learn nothing of the plight of the poor, the changes in politics, the new religious urgency. Jane Austen's England was a closed world in which a very small proportion of the total population participated. One historian has written:

> Both old and new landed gentry were certainly wealthy, happy, and engrossed in the life of their pleasant and beautiful country houses. The war had scarcely upset the delightful routine of their lives.*

They were, in fact, living in a style that had been much the same among their class for centuries. Only the comfort they enjoyed was greater than that of their ancestors.

To a certain extent, the aristocracy was able to control the Church. A living was a position in the clergy, worth varying amounts of money, which an aristocratic patron usually gave accordingly to his or (as in the case of Lady Catherine de Bourgh) her wishes. A would-be clergyman went to one of the two universities—Oxford or Cambridge—after which he fairly easily obtained orders (that is, was ordained† by a Bishop). Even a man of Wickham's dissolute habits could contemplate entering the Church because he had been to Cambridge and his family were patronised by the Darcys, who had a living at their disposal. Thus, clergymen usually came from the aristocracy, the gentry, or its fringes. In the eighteenth century the Church had become very worldly, and Mr Collins may be considered one of its worst examples.

Although the industrial towns of northern England, such as Manchester, Liverpool and Leeds, were growing, southern England remained agricultural. Jane Austen probably never saw the new ugliness and poverty of the north. The England of her novels is still that of eighteenth-century elegance and easy living. Sir William Lucas disengages from trade to enjoy the greater social value of being 'a gentleman'. We only learn in passing that Bingley's father made his fortune in trade in northern England, and his daughters, in their wish to be con-

---

*David Thomson, *England in the Nineteenth Century*, Penguin Books, Harmondsworth, 1950, p.15.

†Ordination is a service of consecration, in which holy orders are conferred upon someone, the ceremony making him a clergyman.

sidered smart and fashionable, conveniently forget it. Social snobbery was quick to seize on inferiority—Darcy is further put off the Bennets because Elizabeth's uncle, Mr Gardiner, has business in Cheapside, which was an unfashionable part of London. Although Mr Bennet was a gentleman, his wife, being the daughter of an attorney, was not from the same 'quality' of family. When Lady de Bourgh is most frustrated and cross with Elizabeth, she describes her as 'a young woman of inferior birth, of no importance in the world'.

But the 'old gentry' was being permeated by the 'new gentry'. Bingley is able to command a position in society because of his large fortune. He is of the new gentry, and hardly has any family roots, since he is still without a family property. In comparison, Darcy comes from an old family and Pemberley has been in its posession for generations. He also has a house in town—in London. This small world with which Jane Austen dealt was established in the countryside, where the gentry had their large houses, and was linked also with the city, where richer gentry and members of the aristocracy often had another house. Mrs Bennet's clash with Darcy over the merits of town people and country people reveals her sense of inferiority—Mr Bennet is of the lesser gentry and has no house in town.

The Bingleys, with a large income, spend the winter months in town and come to Netherfield again in the spring. Darcy's housekeeper informs us that he normally spends six months in the year away from Pemberley. The Bennets, however, permanently reside a mile from Meryton, a small country town. According to Mrs Bennet they have a very good social life ('I know we dine with four and twenty families').

This was the kind of society Jane Austen knew well. We have seen that her father and two of her brothers were clergymen. She wrote about what she knew best with intelligent objectivity. Her values were those of her class, but she was also an author, and had read a good deal of eighteenth-century literature. That period is often referred to as Classical or Neoclassical (because it revived the cultural values of ancient Greece and Rome), while the era that followed it is known as the Romantic era. Jane Austen herself actually lived into the Romantic era.

In simple terms, this Neoclassical outlook was based upon accepted rules—there must be order, proportion, and, above all, reason must control the passions. This was certainly Jane Austen's creed as a writer. We could say that her social beliefs—those of the class to which she belonged—were strengthened by her literary inclinations. At the same time as her novels were being published Keats (1795–1821), Shelley (1792–1822), and Byron (1788–1824) were beginning their careers as poets. They are called Romantics because their poetry stresses passionate feeling and their imagination deals with subjects unusual in everyday life. The eighteenth century, however, had not been completely ruled by order and reason. A tendency towards expressing emotions in literature had developed in the novels, which have been called sentimental and gothic. These novels were often lacking in good taste, and sometimes dealt with very unnatural situations. Heroines were made to undergo severe ordeals and to display violent emotion. A fashion for the remote world of the Christian Middle Ages led to the introduction of castles and ruins, and plots were generally very unreal and fantastic. Authors tried to create a feeling of excitment or even horror. When Jane Austen started to write as a girl she was very satirical about such gothic novels, and wrote mock-sentimental stories. This shows that she was against what was unreal and over-passionate from the very beginning.

The Neoclassical philosophy of the eighteenth century was really a mixture of Christian morality and rationalism. Rationalism—a belief in human reason—was supported by the study of Greek and Roman writers. In eighteenth-century art and philosophy it was believed that underlying the universe were a set of laws which could be understood by man's reason. Also, in men's everyday lives, there were laws which were rational and good. Both sets of laws—those governing the universe, and those governing man—were made by God. The Christian religion was shown to be a set of laws which all good and reasonable men should follow. It was even said by some that the Christian religion only taught what reasonable men would have been able to reason out and follow if it had never existed.

Jane Austen seems to have believed in reason, 'good sense', and the Christian religion. She also accepted, more or less, the beliefs of her social class. We shall see when we come to deal with her literary themes —her way of looking at people and life—how her beliefs appear in her novels.

What can be summarised so far from our discussion of Jane Austen's world is this:

(a) She was brought up in an intelligent but restricted environment. She only knew how a very small section of humanity lived.
(b) Her background was that of the lesser gentry who lived in the country in comfortable pleasant surroundings.
(c) She kept to the values of the eighteenth century—order, reason and good sense.
(d) She was opposed to the values of sentimental or gothic novels, which she herself satirised.

A note on the text

The novel was initially called 'First Impressions', the first draft being produced in the years 1796-7. It was probably written in the same epistolary style as 'Elinor and Marianne', the novel which became *Sense and Sensibility*. Jane Austen was a young woman of twenty-one at this time, but when *Pride and Prejudice* was published she was thirty-seven. Scholars cannot say for certain when the author revised her story. If it was an early revision (some have said 1799–1802), its author was still a young woman. If it was revised between 1811 and 1812, as others suggest, we can say the finished work came from the pen of a mature writer. The first edition was published by T. Egerton, London, in January 1813, a second edition appeared in November 1813, and a third, in two volumes, in 1817.

The first edition is the best text. It needs a correction which Jane Austen pointed out (in it two speeches were made into one, on p.220, V.3) and some printers' errors have to be eliminated. The text edited by R. W. Chapman, Clarendon Press, Oxford, 1923, is followed by modern editions. Among them are the Everyman edition, edited with an Introduction by Mary Lascelles, Dent, London, revised edition, 1963, and the Penguin English Library edition, edited with an Introduction by Tony Tanner, Penguin Books, Harmondsworth, 1972 (Tanner departs from Chapman's text in two small points).

All references in these Notes are to the edition published by Oxford University Press, Oxford, 1970.

Part 2

Summaries
of PRIDE AND PREJUDICE

A general summary

News reaches the Bennet family of Longbourn, Hertfordshire, that a rich, eligible young man is moving into the neighbourhood. Mrs Bennet, anxious to get her five daughters well married, insists that her husband should go to Netherfield, the house to be rented by Mr Bingley, and make his acquaintance. Mr Bennet does this, but takes pleasure in tantalising his wife and daughters by telling them in a round-about way.

Mr Bingley calls briefly soon after. We learn that he is interested in the Bennet girls. He is to see them at a ball in Meryton, the local country town. He soon finds the prettiest one to be Jane, the eldest. During the evening he shows her special favours. Meanwhile, we are introduced to his friend, Mr Darcy. It is rumoured that he is a very rich man. But his manners, which are proud and aloof, earn him the bad opinion of most persons. He only dances with Mr Bingley's sisters, and makes a haughty remark about Elizabeth, the second Bennet daughter, which she overhears.

The attachment of Jane and Mr Bingley causes his sisters to make friends with her. Mr Darcy, in the meantime, begins to discover that Elizabeth is attractive, and not just 'tolerable', as he had said at the ball. They meet at a party at the home of Sir William Lucas and the pattern of their relationship is set: Darcy courts Elizabeth in his own, apparently brusque manner; she, thinking he disapproves of her, responds with irony and humour. This further captivates Darcy.

Mr Bingley is now very attracted to Jane. His sisters invite her to Netherfield although Mr Bingley is away that evening. Mrs Bennet contrives to secure an invitation for Jane to stay the night there by sending her on horseback, knowing it will rain and she will be unable to return. But Jane catches a cold and has to stay even longer. Elizabeth, who is very close to her sister, walks the three miles to Netherfield to find out how she is. This startles the ladies, and the gentlemen, who have since returned. When Elizabeth is with her sister, the Bingley sisters criticise Jane's relatives and especially Elizabeth's behaviour.

During Jane's illness, Elizabeth stays at Netherfield. Mr Darcy enters into several conversations with her and they seem to disagree. Miss Bingley, however, wants Darcy for herself, and can see that he is interested in Elizabeth. She tries to ingratiate herself with Darcy by consistently praising his opinions. But Darcy is by now quite drawn to Elizabeth despite the apparent friction between them. He resolves, however, not to pay her further attention. He is strengthened in this decision by his realisation that her relations are of low social standing.

The estate of Mr Bennet is entailed to a male nephew. (This means that it must pass to a male heir and his daughters cannot inherit his property when he dies.) The Reverend Collins is this nephew, and he comes to visit Longbourn. He wishes to marry one of the Bennet girls, as he has heard of their beauty, and has been advised by his patroness, Lady Catherine de Bourgh, to obtain a wife. He proves to be a shallow, materialistic man, made ridiculous by his pompous manners and his exaggerated praise of Lady Catherine.

Lydia and Kitty, Mrs Bennet's younger daughters, are, like her, frivolous and empty. They like to go often to Meryton where Mrs Bennet's sister, Mrs Philips, lives. But their main object is to see the officers of the county militia who are quartered in Meryton. On one trip, which includes Elizabeth, Jane and Mr Collins, the party meets a Mr George Wickham, who is accompanying one of the officers. At the same time, Darcy and Bingley pass by. At Mrs Philips's house, Elizabeth becomes Wickham's particular object. His smooth manners win over everyone, and Elizabeth makes her greatest error of judgement in mistaking his superficiality for sincerity. That he is somehow known to Darcy she realises because of the strained recognition they had shown to each other when they met in Meryton. Wickham tells Elizabeth that Darcy had ruined his career prospects by denying him the living which Darcy's father had destined for Wickham, who was the son of his steward.

Mr Bingley holds a ball. Although invited, Wickham does not attend. This prejudices Elizabeth even further against Darcy. But she still dances with him. The Bennet family, however, make a bad showing. The pedantic Mary Bennet shows her bad taste in singing too much; Mr Bennet deals awkwardly with her; and Mrs Bennet talks loudly about Jane marrying Bingley. Darcy sees and hears all this, and has to bear Mr Collins's pompous introduction of himself as Lady Catherine's beneficiary. It is revealed later that this display of the Bennets settles Darcy in his resolution to take Bingley away from Netherfield—and the Bennets. He feels he must forget Elizabeth and that Bingley must forget Jane. The Netherfield party leave soon afterwards for London. Jane hears from Miss Bingley that they do not expect to return. Though she tries to hide it, she is very upset, and her mother's worrying only makes it worse.

Mrs Bennet is by this time very nervous and irritable. Mr Collins, directed by her to Elizabeth, has proposed marriage. Elizabeth refused. Mr Collins persisted but Mr Bennet supported his daughter. Soon after, Collins proposes to Charlotte Lucas, daughter of Sir William and a friend of Elizabeth. Being plain looking, she accepts the first offer of marriage made to her, for another is not likely. This makes Mrs Bennet very irritable indeed.

At Christmas, Jane goes to London to visit her Uncle Gardiner, Mrs Bennet's brother. Wickham has blackened Darcy's name throughout the neighbourhood, and, although he switches his attentions to an heiress, Elizabeth still supports his story against Darcy. By March, Jane is resigned to losing Mr Bingley, and sees the hypocrisy of his sister. Miss Bingley visits Jane only once in London. She lets Jane know that Bingley and Miss Darcy are likely to marry.

Meanwhile, Elizabeth visits Charlotte at Hunsford, in Kent, with Sir William and his daughter. They dine with Lady Catherine de Bourgh, who likes to overwhelm everyone with her rank and importance. Soon her nephews, Darcy, and a Colonel Fitzwilliam, arrive to stay. Elizabeth likes Fitzwilliam and he likes her, but he must marry a woman with money. Darcy comes to the parsonage often, and one day finds Elizabeth alone. He also meets her often when she goes for her walks. All this surprises her, and though Charlotte believes Darcy is in love, she too finds his silent manner strange.

At last Darcy overcomes his prejudice against the Bennet family, so strongly does he love Elizabeth. But when he comes to propose marriage she is already upset and ill with a headache. Earlier that day, Colonel Fitzwilliam had told her enough for her to realise that Darcy's influence had ruined Jane's chances with Bingley. To add to this disadvantage, Darcy seems to expect that Elizabeth will accept him. He says too much about the objections he has had to overcome before he could propose to her. Elizabeth is now most angry at this display of Darcy's pride. She refuses him, giving as her reasons his proud emphasis on her inferiority, his part in separating Jane and Bingley, and his treatment of Wickham. Having hurt Elizabeth's pride, Darcy now has his own hurt. He leaves in subdued anger.

Darcy sets out his explanations in a letter to Elizabeth which he gives her personally next day. Elizabeth reads it at first with strong prejudice. However, Darcy's account of his dealings with Wickham strongly affect her. After reading the letter several times, she is ashamed of her prejudice for Wickham and against Darcy, and even sees that Darcy had good reasons for separating Jane and Bingley.

With changed feelings towards Darcy, Elizabeth goes to Derbyshire with the Gardiners for a tour. She knows that Darcy had fully lived up to his responsibility for Wickham, but that Wickham had behaved abominably by leading an immoral life. He had demanded the living which he had previously renounced for cash, and then attempted to seduce Darcy's fifteen-year-old sister. Also, she now sees how badly her parents have brought up the family. Lydia was now in Brighton, despite Elizabeth's advice to her father to stop her going, and Wickham was also there, having left with the militia.

In Derbyshire, Elizabeth and her aunt and uncle visit Pemberley. They are told by Darcy's housekeeper of his many qualities. Although nervous, Elizabeth believes Darcy is not due back until the next day. However, he comes back early and they meet by accident. Although embarrassed, he is civil, and a little later meets them again, and is introduced to her aunt and uncle. Elizabeth is surprised by the change in Darcy. He is now courteous, and wishes to please. Darcy is surprised by the good taste of Elizabeth's relatives. In a short time, the way is prepared for a renewal of Darcy's proposal. Elizabeth is introduced to Miss Darcy, who is shy, and meets the Bingleys again. Miss Bingley, now completely powerless, still abuses Elizabeth.

Then comes sudden news of Lydia's elopement with Wickham. Elizabeth breaks down and Darcy finds her crying. She tells him all she knows, bitterly reproaching herself for not having exposed Wickham's true character. Darcy leaves. Elizabeth, feeling gratitude and respect, had thought she might marry him. Now she believes this to be hopeless. She returns home to find her mother confined to her room in a nervous state, and Mr Bennet gone to London, where Lydia and Wickham are thought to be. Elizabeth hardly believes that Wickham will marry Lydia, although Jane still hopes so. News comes of Wickham's debts in Meryton and Brighton. Mr Bennet returns with nothing achieved. But suddenly the clouds lift; Mr Gardiner writes to say that Wickham has been found and will marry Lydia. Mrs Bennet turns from depression to irresponsible joy. Both Mr Bennet and Elizabeth believe that Wickham has been paid a large amount of money by Mr Gardiner.

Mr Bennet is forced to let the couple come to Longbourn before going to settle in the north. Both are the same as ever, and entirely unrepentant. Lydia mentions that Darcy was at the wedding and Elizabeth receives the whole story from her aunt in a letter. Darcy had known where to find the couple in London, and had paid Wickham a good marriage settlement. He had wished his part in it all to remain secret, and gave as his motive his fault for not exposing Wickham's true character.

The Wickhams leave and Bingley and Darcy return. Now unrestrained by his friend, Bingley soon renews his attachment with Jane. Mrs Bennet also renews her scheming. Darcy, however, is silent and withdrawn when he visits. Elizabeth, her hopes revived by her knowledge of his help of Lydia, now fears them mistaken. The inevitable happens when Bingley proposes to Jane. Then occurs the surprise visit of Lady Catherine de Bourgh. She wishes to frighten Elizabeth away from Darcy, for she has heard of their engagement from Mr Collins.

She claims that Darcy is engaged to Miss de Bourgh, her sickly daughter. But Elizabeth, realising the weakness of Lady Catherine's arguments, refuses to give any ground. Later, Darcy confirms that his Aunt's visit had helped him to make up his mind to ask Elizabeth again, for, having failed with Elizabeth, Lady Catherine went to try to dissuade her nephew. But to prepare Elizabeth for the reaction of her family to their possible engagement, we see Mr Bennet ridicule a letter from Mr Collins that congratulates him on the match. So strange is such a union in the eyes of Elizabeth's family.

However, Mrs Bennet's schemes unknowingly bring Elizabeth and Darcy together. She sends them out on a walk and Elizabeth thanks Darcy for his help of Lydia. He says it was all done on Elizabeth's account and renews his vow of affection. Now Elizabeth can tell him the change in her own affections, and they share mutual confessions and apologies for past guilt.

Jane is the first to be surprised by news of the engagement. Mr Bennet, thinking of his own marriage, advises Elizabeth not to marry without love. But Mrs Bennet, in the quickest change of heart in the novel, turns from thinking Mr Darcy 'disagreeable' to finding him 'such a charming man'. All that is left are the explanations for Darcy's recent behaviour, and his sufferance of Elizabeth's relatives. The novel ends with a summary of the future of all the main characters. The eldest sisters enjoy happy marriages and live far away from their mother. Lydia bothers them both for financial help. Kitty, Miss Darcy, and the Gardiners all derive pleasure from Mr and Mrs Darcy; whilst Lady Catherine, after making war on her nephew and his wife, finally makes peace.

Detailed summaries

Volume 1: Chapter 1

The Bennets discuss the expected arrival of Mr Bingley, the new tenant of Netherfield. He is 'a young man of fortune from the north of England'. Mrs Bennet wants her husband to make his acquaintance before her neighbours because she hopes Mr Bingley will marry one of her daughters. Mr Bennet is ironic and pretends not to understand. His wife prefers Jane and Lydia, but Mr Bennet's favourite is Elizabeth.

COMMENTARY: In the famous opening sentence of the novel, Jane Austen is making an ironic suggestion that the families in the society she wrote about were always looking for rich husbands to whom they could marry their daughters. Mrs Bennet is an extreme example, but we hear that others—Mrs Long and the Lucases—are also interested. Mr Bennet must first call on Mr Bingley to make his acquaintance because this is social etiquette—or what is done in 'society'. Mr Bennet pretends not to understand this, but secretly intends to visit Bingley. The last paragraph sums up the whole chapter.

Chapter 2

Mr Bennet does visit Mr Bingley but does not tell his wife. He is ironic about Kitty's coughing and Mary's learning. On rousing his wife's interest about Mr Bingley, he purposely confuses her. He then matter-of-factly reveals the news of his visit. This receives the astonishment for which he had wished.

COMMENTARY: Mr Bennet uses the kind of arguments Mrs Bennet would use to perplex his wife and daughters on the subject of getting to know Mr Bingley. We see that Mr Bennet is far more intelligent than his wife. She is irritable with everyone because she cannot have her way over Mr Bingley, but when she realises Mr Bennet has done what she wants, her mood is completely changed. This is characteristic of Mrs Bennet. So too are Lydia's first remarks ending: 'though I *am* the youngest, I am the tallest'.

Chapter 3

Mr Bingley repays Mr Bennet's call and then goes to London to fetch a group for the ball. Bingley and his friends are the talking-point of everyone there. First of all, Mr Darcy is thought to be even more eligible than Bingley, for he is richer and owns a large estate in Derbyshire. But he only dances with Bingley's sisters and when Bingley tries to make him dance with another lady, Darcy remarks that, in Jane, Bingley has the most beautiful partner to himself. Bingley points out Elizabeth but Darcy says: 'She is tolerable; but not handsome enough to tempt *me*.' Elizabeth overhears his remarks, but is able to laugh about them with her friends. Mrs Bennet is overjoyed because Bingley dances twice with Jane, but tells Mr Bennet that she detests Darcy for being too proud to dance with Elizabeth.

COMMENTARY: We see how money and beauty are valued in Jane Austen's world. She satirises the opinions of its inhabitants by making them into apparently serious truths: 'To be fond of dancing was a certain step towards falling in love.' Then she adds: 'and very lively hopes of Mr Bingley's heart were entertained'. He is both handsome, amicable and rich. He is attracted immediately to Jane as the most beautiful girl. Mrs Bennet thinks it inevitable. But at the same time, we see the beginning of a more complex relationship. Darcy is rich and handsome, but too proud to lower himself. His dismissal of Elizabeth is very ironic, for later her beauty captivates him. She is no ordinary heroine, but a lively, intelligent girl. On their first meeting, the two major characters make a bad start with each other. They do not fall in love at first sight as do lovers in sentimental novels.

Chapter 4

Jane Austen shows more closely the characters she has introduced. Elizabeth and Jane discuss the ball, and chiefly Mr Bingley. Jane is modest and thinks well of everyone, including Bingley's two sisters. Elizabeth does not approve of them. We learn more about Bingley's background. He inherits his fortune from his father who had made it in trade, but he is too easy-going to invest it in an estate. Bingley is very pleased with his new neighbours. Darcy sees only their deficiencies.

COMMENTARY: There is irony in the author's remark about Bingley's background. The two sisters try not to remember that their brother's fortune was made in trade. Although they are fashionable, they are empty people. In thinking Jane 'a sweet girl', we can see that their attitude is superior and patronising. The contrast between Bingley and Darcy is established.

NOTES AND GLOSSARY:
candid: Jane Austen uses this word to mean 'free from finding faults'
liberty of the manor: means Bingley had the shooting rights

Chapter 5

The Lucases are introduced. The ball is still the subject of conversation. Elizabeth and Charlotte are intimate friends. We see how Mrs Bennet is still glorying in Jane's success, and how Jane cannot believe ill of Mr Darcy. We also see how Elizabeth can be light-hearted over the bad behaviour of Darcy toward herself.

COMMENTARY: Sir William Lucas has risen up the social ladder and, like the Bingley sisters, wishes to forget his connections with trade. His daughter, Charlotte, is 'sensible' and 'intelligent'. However, Lady Lucas is as small-minded as Mrs Bennet. Mrs Bennet's quarrel with the Lucas boy shows again how small-minded she is. She argues with the child at his own level of intelligence.

Chapter 6

The 'friendship' of the Bingley sisters and Jane continues, but it is merely because of their brother's feeling for her. Jane is so composed that she does not show her preference for Bingley. Charlotte and Elizabeth discuss the couple. Charlotte believes Jane should show more than she feels so as 'to help on' Bingley. Elizabeth says Jane cannot by nature act with such motives. Charlotte does not have a high view of marriage. A happy marriage is for her just a question of chance.

At the Lucases' party, Darcy, having studied Elizabeth more, recognises her charms, especially 'the beautiful expression of her dark eyes'. By now he is very happy to dance with Elizabeth, unlike at the first ball. Elizabeth behaves archly, however, and refuses when Sir William Lucas suggests it. Darcy tells Miss Bingley that he has been admiring Elizabeth's eyes. Miss Bingley reminds him of her relatives. Darcy had earlier been angered by the bad taste of Mary Bennet and her young sisters.

COMMENTARY: Charlotte's words on marriage present an apparently practical, unromantic view of it. Elizabeth laughs at her and does not think she is serious. Elizabeth's judgement proves wrong, and she is disappointed when Charlotte later acts according to her words.

The party shows how things are likely to develop: Elizabeth's liveliness and intelligent wit unintentionally attract Darcy, but the ignorance of her family is already plain to him. Miss Bingley, being jealous, is only too ready to remind him of it.

Chapter 7

Mr Bennet's property is entailed and will not be inherited by any of his daughters. Mr Bennet and Mrs Bennet disagree over the intelligence of Lydia and Kitty, who are always running after the officers in the militia stationed in Meryton. They take after Mrs Bennet who once liked soldiers herself and encourages her daughters in their behaviour.

Miss Bingley invites Jane to dinner in her brother's absence; and Mrs Bennet sends her on horseback, thinking it will rain so that Jane must then stay overnight. News comes next morning that Jane has caught cold. Elizabeth anxiously walks the three miles to Netherfield, causing great surprise when she arrives at breakfast time.

COMMENTARY: Mrs Bennet unknowingly prepares the way for Lydia's elopement with Wickham. Seen in this way, her words are quite ironic: 'and if a smart young colonel, with five or six thousand a year, should want one of my girls, I shall not say nay to him.' She is clever in sending Jane on horseback so as to be detained but, as we see later, her schemes are always embarrassingly obvious in the way they are carried out.

Elizabeth shows how unconventional a heroine she is in walking so far, and even jumping over stiles on the way. Although this shocks the genteel ladies, it adds to Darcy's interest in her.

Chapter 8

Elizabeth sees how hypocritical is the regard of the Bingley sisters for Jane. They soon forget her illness despite their assurances of sympathy. Mr Hurst lives only to eat and play cards. Miss Bingley criticises Elizabeth severely when she is out of the room. Bingley defends Jane and Elizabeth against her criticism of their relatives. Although Darcy is further attracted to Elizabeth by her walk, he accepts that the inferiority of their relatives in social standing will hinder Jane and Elizabeth making good marriages.

Darcy and Miss Bingley appear to have the same opinions on social refinements, and Elizabeth disagrees with them over the accomplishments that a lady must have.

COMMENTARY: Although Darcy appears to agree with the social judgements of Miss Bingley, the attraction of Elizabeth is already causing a change in him. Miss Bingley's way of trying to attract Darcy is to praise him, but she does this too obviously. Elizabeth shows her independent judgement by challenging both of them.

Chapter 9

Mrs Bennet comes to see Jane and, of course, will not have her moved. In her conversation, she makes very obvious innuendos about Jane and Bingley. Elizabeth says she understands Bingley's character and that she likes to study character in general. Darcy thinks the country is too limited for doing this, but Mrs Bennet angrily argues that the country is as good as the town. In doing so, her dislike of Mr Darcy is very obvious and her own conceit quite embarrassing for Elizabeth. Before Mrs Bennet leaves, Lydia reminds Mr Bingley that he has promised to give a ball.

COMMENTARY: The character of Mrs Bennet is further displayed. She lets her tongue voice her thoughts without restraint, criticising Darcy, and comparing Charlotte Lucas unfavourably with Jane. Jane Austen does not make her do this simply for effect. All the while the plot is being developed. Mrs Bennet's stupidity and Elizabeth's attractiveness create a tension in the story. Darcy is held between his contempt for the mother and admiration of the daughter.

A careful examination of the discussions of character provided in the novel will help us to understand Jane Austen's attitude to her writing. For example, her own views seem to be placed in the mouth of Elizabeth: 'But people themselves alter so much, that there is something new to be observed in them for ever.'

Chapter 10

Miss Bingley continues to praise Darcy. Elizabeth and Darcy develop a discussion on the subject of Bingley's hastiness and easy compliance with the wishes of friends. Bingley dislikes the argument and makes a joke at Darcy's expense. While Miss Bingley plays the piano Darcy watches Elizabeth intently. She believes this is because he in some way disapproves of her, but she does not care. Again, he asks her to dance, but she refuses, thinking he is trying to catch her out. But Miss Bingley is jealous of Darcy's attention to Elizabeth. She makes ironic remarks about Elizabeth's relatives and her eyes, because she wants to ridicule a possible marriage between Darcy and Elizabeth.

COMMENTARY: In the discussion between Elizabeth and Darcy there is some irony, for they talk about Bingley's sudden departure from Netherfield and the influence of a friend upon him. Later, Bingley does leave Netherfield on Darcy's advice. This scene reveals character in a masterly way. Elizabeth matches Darcy in intelligent discussion, and, in refusing to dance a reel, only interests him the more. Bingley is mystified about what is going on, but his sister, sensing Darcy's feelings, tries to slight Elizabeth. But when she and Mrs Hurst are rude to Elizabeth by leaving her to walk by herself, Elizabeth reacts to Darcy's politeness by making a witty remark and hurrying away. We feel the attractiveness of her lively, individual personality.

Chapter 11

The triangle involving Darcy, Miss Bingley and Elizabeth continues. Miss Bingley first tries to gain Darcy's good opinion by expressing what she imagines are his views on the coming Netherfield ball. Next, in order to attract his attention, she gets up and walks around. In desperation, she invites Elizabeth to do the same. Darcy does look up then. Another conversation develops between Darcy and Elizabeth on human faults. Elizabeth likes to ridicule folly, but not what is wise or good. Darcy says he has always tried to avoid folly himself. Elizabeth's answer seems to accuse him of pride, and he finally admits: his 'temper' is 'too little yielding'; his 'good opinion once lost is lost forever'. Elizabeth playfully replies that this is a fault too serious to be laughed at. Miss Bingley finally ends the repartee by calling for music. But Darcy is even further attracted to Elizabeth.

COMMENTARY: Jane Austen's use of dialogue is shown here at its most subtle. Darcy and Elizabeth discuss each other's faults, and in both we see errors of judgement. Elizabeth seems to expose Darcy's pride, but all the while she is unaware of his growing affection for her. Darcy is right in saying Elizabeth is wilfully misunderstanding him, but wrong in defending his pride. Miss Bingley cannot understand any of this and only wishes to end their conversation.

Chapter 12

Despite Mrs Bennet's obstructions, Jane and Elizabeth return home. Darcy is relieved because Elizabeth attracts him 'more than he liked'.

COMMENTARY: The stay of Jane and Elizabeth at Netherfield has enabled them to get to know the two men who are to court and eventually marry them.

Chapter 13

Mr Bennet informs his wife and daughters of the imminent arrival of Mr Collins, who had written a month ago. His letter is pompous in style, and hints that he is coming to Longbourn with a proposal in mind. Elizabeth sees that the writer 'must be an oddity', while Mr Bennet hopes he will be. Mr Collins arrives and behaves with formality and ceremony, remarking on the beauty of the Bennet girls, and praising Longbourn.

COMMENTARY: Mr Collins proves to be as his letter had warned. He does everything with awkward formality. He writes about the duties he must perform for his patron, Lady Catherine de Bourgh. Even the Church seems to come second to these. His approach to courtship is along the same lines: 'I can assure the young ladies that I come prepared to admire them.'

Chapter 14

Mr Collins describes how he is used to complimenting Lady Catherine and her daughter. Mr Bennet satirically asks if he prepares his speeches beforehand. When asked to read to the Bennets, Collins chooses a book of sermons especially written for young ladies. Lydia shows her bad manners by interrupting him with her empty chatter.

COMMENTARY: Mr Bennet is delighted by Mr Collins's absurdity, and his question about Mr Collins's speeches is so dryly humorous that Collins completely misses its sarcasm.

Chapter 15

Mr Collins, we are told, is not a sensible man. His education has had little good effect. His nature is 'a mixture of pride and obsequiousness, self importance and humility'. The change of his admiration, from Jane to Elizabeth, shows he is completely without deeper feeling. Mrs Bennet encourages him in this.

The girls walk to Meryton with Mr Collins. They are introduced to George Wickham by a fellow officer. Bingley and Darcy ride by, and there is a very strained recognition between Darcy and Wickham. Mrs Philips, the sister of Mrs Bennet, welcomes her nieces and is 'quite awed' by the manners of Mr Collins.

COMMENTARY: Jane Austen accurately sums up the shallow nature of Mr Collins. Mr Bennet soon tires of him and is happy to see him walk to Meryton with his daughters. The strange meeting of Darcy and Wickham is noticed only by Elizabeth. We see that Mrs Philips is no more intelligent than Mrs Bennet.

Chapter 16

Elizabeth meets Wickham at her Aunt Philips's. She is curious to know about his relation to Darcy, and Wickham is the first to mention the subject. He tells her that Darcy had gone against his father's wishes in not giving Wickham the clerical living which had originally been intended for him. Elizabeth easily accepts Wickham's story. Wickham advances jealousy as Darcy's motive. He says Darcy is proud, although he can be generous to his family and servants. Wickham's story is more believable in the eyes of Elizabeth because of his attractive manners. She learns that Lady Catherine de Bourgh is Darcy's aunt, and that she hopes to join her estate with Pemberley by the marriage of Darcy with her daughter.

COMMENTARY: Elizabeth is won over by the outward appearance of Wickham. So smooth are his manners, and so handsome is he in appearance, that she believes all he tells her, although she ought to have realised how indiscreet he is to speak about such matters to a person he hardly knows. She hastily judges Darcy entirely on the value of Wickham's story. 'This is quite shocking!—He deserves to be publicly disgraced,' she says. If we study Wickham's speech, we see how cunning a villain he is.

NOTES AND GLOSSARY:
fish: a counter used in games

Chapter 17

Elizabeth tells Wickham's story to Jane. Jane is so far from thinking badly of anyone that she thinks both men must have been deceived. She will not believe Bingley could be friends with Darcy otherwise.

Miss Bingley arrives with an invitation to the Netherfield ball. Elizabeth, in her pleasant anticipations, asks Mr Collins if he will go, thinking a ball might be against his scruples. He surprises her so much as to ask her for the first two dances which she had intended to dance with Wickham. She soon realises that Mr Collins is interested in her.

COMMENTARY: Jane refuses to think badly of anyone, whereas Elizabeth is too quick to acquire a prejudice against Darcy. Jane is no more perceptive than Elizabeth, for she never sees the bad in human beings. Elizabeth has better judgement, but has to learn to be careful of letting her prejudice mar it. She is too lively in dealing with Collins and this only serves to encourage him in what she least wants—a proposal of marriage.

Chapter 18

Elizabeth expects to conquer Wickham's heart entirely at the ball. But he does not come, and she immediately blames Darcy. Her dances with Mr Collins spoil her evening further, for he makes mistakes and keeps apologising. Then Darcy asks her to dance. So surprised is she that she accepts. Charlotte advises her not to hinder Mr Darcy's attentions. But Elizabeth is determined to hate him. When they dance, she mentions Wickham and gets a cold response. Meanwhile, Jane is getting on very well with Bingley. But the Bennet family soon undoes the advantage of Jane's beauty. Mary sings too much, Mr Bennet is too obvious in stopping her, and Mrs Bennet speaks loudly about Jane and Bingley marrying. Even Mr Collins makes matters worse by introducing himself pompously to Darcy.

COMMENTARY: This chapter is a turning point in the novel. The bad display of the Bennets is too much for Darcy and it results in his taking Bingley away from Netherfield. The previous effects of the charms of Jane and Elizabeth on the two friends are seemingly undone.

Chapter 19

Backed by the efforts of Mrs Bennet, Mr Collins proposes marriage to Elizabeth. His proposal gives lengthy details of his reasons for marrying and he assumes Elizabeth will accept him. Her refusal surprises him, but he attributes it to the natural ways of women. Elizabeth refuses again more clearly, but he still believes she is behaving as elegant ladies behave. His attempts to be gallant add more humour to the situation.

COMMENTARY: This excellent example of Jane Austen's humour is further evidence of her genius for inventing character and situation. It is full of irony: here is an absurdly formal clergyman acting as a passionate lover. He says: 'but before I am run away with by my feelings on this subject', and then proceeds to talk about Lady Catherine de Bourgh. It is also ironic that such a clergyman should make allowance for female coquetry. Elizabeth, in contrast, denies that she is behaving like a romantic woman.

Chapter 20

Mr Collins tells Mrs Bennet what he thinks has happened. Mrs Bennet is cross because she knows Elizabeth would not behave with 'bashful modesty', and realises she has refused him. She calls her a 'very head-strong foolish girl', which makes Mr Collins, already puzzled, unsure that he wants such a person as his wife.

Mr Bennet hears of the matter and calls his wife and daughter into the library. He directly and humorously opposes his wife by not con-senting to the marriage. Mrs Bennet does not give in, but, at this dramatic time, Charlotte Lucas arrives and spends the day with Collins. Elizabeth is thankful to her for taking up his attention. Mr Collins makes a speech on the need for resignation, and avows the purity of his motives.

COMMENTARY: Jane Austen excels in comedy with the two ridiculous characters, Collins and Mrs Bennet, performing together. Mr Bennet's sarcasm might be taken for her own voice in the matter. The arrival of Charlotte at such a time is ironic, for she draws Mr Collins's attentions to herself, while Elizabeth thanks her for the trouble. Mrs Bennet reveals all her fustration in a long, meandering speech of complaint to Elizabeth.

Chapter 21

Mr Collins shows 'resentful silence' to Elizabeth. She goes with her sisters to Meryton and meets Wickham, who tells her he stayed away from the ball because of Darcy. Jane receives a letter from Miss Bingley informing her of their departure from Netherfield and intention not to return. She drops obvious hints that Bingley and Darcy's sister will become engaged. Elizabeth tells her sister that these are only Miss Bingley's wishes and that Bingley will return: Miss Bingley only sees that her brother loves Jane and wishes to keep him in London. Jane still believes Miss Bingley could not wish to do such a thing.

COMMENTARY: Elizabeth is sympathetic to Wickham and likes the compliment of being singled out by him. She sees that Bingley has been influenced by someone and thinks it is his sister but she is confident of his love for Jane.

Chapter 22

Miss Lucas encourages Mr Collins and after a very short time he proposes to her and is accepted. Charlotte only wishes to marry him for the house and comforts he can offer. She has no respect for him and therefore wishes a short courtship and speedy marriage. The Lucases are delighted by the match and begin to think of their daughter living at Longbourn when Collins inherits it. Elizabeth is shocked that Charlotte 'would have sacrificed every better feeling to worldly advantage', and believes she cannot be happy with Collins.

COMMENTARY: Jane Austen develops her satiric picture of Collins as a lover. He shows 'fire and independence' in going to Lucas Lodge to 'throw himself' at Charlotte's feet. He still makes long speeches and Charlotte quickly accepts him for fear of any more. This chapter shows Jane Austen at her most hard and realistic. Mr Collins's stupidity is clearly exposed and Charlotte's worldly reasons for marrying are clearly set out.

Chapter 23

Sir William Lucas is badly received by the Bennets when he comes with the news of the engagement. Mrs Bennet, when she can bring herself to believe it, takes the news very badly. Mr Bennet's reaction is cynical—he is happy to see Charlotte Lucas is as foolish as his wife. The intimacy between Charlotte and Elizabeth is marred. Mr Collins returns to Longbourn after going to get Lady Catherine's consent. Bingley's absence becomes more worrying than Elizabeth had thought at first.

COMMENTARY: Most of the characters show in their behaviour much human selfishness. Collins comes to Longbourn a second time without any thought for the Bennets. Mrs Bennet is upset because all her plans are ruined and she hates to think of Charlotte inheriting Longbourn. Elizabeth even begins to doubt Bingley. Her view of human nature is disappointed by Charlotte's mercenary engagement.

Volume 2: Chapter 1

Another letter from Miss Bingley settles that Bingley will not return to Netherfield and repeats the story of his probable engagement to Miss Darcy. Elizabeth thinks Bingley is weak in allowing others to influence him like this. Jane's hopes are destroyed, but she behaves angelically, in her sister's eyes. When Elizabeth laments the behaviour of Charlotte, Jane still believes the marriage can be a happy one. She defends Bingley's inconstancy by saying he could not have been attached to her. If this were true, his sisters and Darcy could not be blamed for wanting him to marry Miss Darcy. She must have hoped for too much because of Bingley's attentions.

Mrs Bennet becomes more depressed by Bingley's behaviour.

Darcy's treatment of Wickham is known everywhere in the district. Only Jane refuses to condemn Darcy.

COMMENTARY: The series of disappointments give Elizabeth a dark view of human beings. Mr Bennet is too cynical about them to care any longer, and he jokes about Jane being jilted. Although she is well aware that people behave inconsistently and with poor judgement, Elizabeth still keeps her high ideals of marriage.

Chapter 2

Mr Collins leaves Hertfordshire. The Gardiners visit Longbourn. Mr Gardiner is the brother of Mrs Bennet, but is better bred and more intelligent than his sisters, although in trade. Mrs Gardiner is close to Jane and Elizabeth, and is able to discuss Jane's misfortunes sensibly. She invites her to London, where Jane believes she might meet Miss Bingley as a friend. Mrs Gardiner notices the warmth between Wickham and Elizabeth. She likes him immediately because he comes from the same part of Derbyshire as herself.

COMMENTARY: The Gardiners, as Elizabeth's only sensible relatives, play an influential part in the novel. Mrs Gardiner is able to discuss Jane's misfortunes in a way Mrs Bennet could not. She is also a welcome companion for Elizabeth. However, even Mrs Gardiner is ready to accept the dark picture of Darcy's character spread about by Wickham.

Chapter 3

Mrs Gardiner advises Elizabeth to guard against falling in love with Wickham because of his lack of fortune. A little later Wickham himself makes the advice unnecessary by pursuing an heiress and dropping his attentions to Elizabeth.

Charlotte marries Mr Collins and makes Elizabeth promise to visit her at her new house in Kent. Jane goes to London. She is finally brought to see that Miss Bingley cares nothing for her.

COMMENTARY: The projected visit of Elizabeth to Kent is important in the development of the plot, for there she will meet Darcy who is visiting his aunt. Elizabeth's judgement is inconsistent over Wickham. Having been disappointed by Charlotte's worldly decision to marry Collins for material reasons alone, she overlooks the same motives in Wickham when he courts a lady with ten thousand pounds.

Chapter 4

Elizabeth sets out for Kent, stopping at her aunt's London house on the way. She defends Wickham's behaviour with Miss King against her aunt's criticism. A tour of the Lake District of northern England is planned by Elizabeth and the Gardiners.

COMMENTARY: Mrs Gardiner warns Elizabeth against 'disappointment'. By this we may understand that Wickham's behaviour, added to that of Charlotte, Bingley, and Darcy, has caused Elizabeth to adopt a bitter manner. For a moment, her visit brings her the closest she gets to the cynicism of her father. However, the prospect of seeing the beauty of the Lake District revives her natural enthusiasm.

Chapter 5

Elizabeth arrives at Hunsford Parsonage with Sir William Lucas and Maria, his daughter. Mr Collins shows off his home with his usual exaggeration and pomposity. Elizabeth thinks he is trying to make her aware of what she has lost by refusing to marry him. Instead she feels sorry for Charlotte. He informs Elizabeth that they will all be invited to Rosings, Lady Catherine's stately home. Maria is overcome with excitement and awe to see Miss de Bourgh and her companion, Mrs Jenkinson. They only stop to deliver an invitation to dinner and do not get out of their carriage. Elizabeth sees their rudeness in making Charlotte stand out in the cold, and thinks Miss de Bourgh sickly looking. She also thinks Miss de Bourgh would suit Darcy.

COMMENTARY: Elizabeth is not to be impressed by Collins's blatant materialism and the self-conscious rank of the de Bourghs. She squashes Maria's wonder by saying: 'And is this all?' . . . 'I expected at least that the pigs were got into the garden, and here is nothing but Lady Catherine and her daughter.'

Chapter 6

The party dine at Rosings. Mr Collins points out each detail that can add to his visitors' appreciation of the wealth and importance of his patroness. He sees not so much the beauty of the park as the number of trees in it.

Sir William and his daughter are completely awed. Lady Catherine makes everyone feel the inferiority of their rank, and dominates the conversation. She gives her opinion on every matter as if it were the only possible one, and asks Elizabeth questions that are too direct and impolite. She is amazed that the Bennet girls had no governess, and that all five daughters go into society at once. Elizabeth, asked how old she is, makes a witty reply. Lady Catherine is not used to such independence of mind.

COMMENTARY: Elizabeth is not overwhelmed by money and rank. Lady Catherine, though she has both, is really an insensitive, badly-mannered woman. Sir William is humorously shown to be an impressionable man who is not at ease in the company of high rank.

Chapter 7

Sir William soon leaves. Elizabeth is relieved whenever Mr Collins leaves their company and sees that Charlotte has arranged the house so that he is near her as little as possible. Elizabeth also learns that Lady Catherine is always ordering the affairs of everybody in the parish.

Darcy arrives with his cousin, Colonel Fitzwilliam, the younger son of a Lord. When they visit the Parsonage, Elizabeth asks Darcy if he has seen Jane in London, knowing he has not. Darcy replies with a little confusion, implying he knew Jane was there.

COMMENTARY: Elizabeth again asks a direct question of Darcy, trying to give him a sense of guilt. She had done this at the Netherfield ball when she mentioned Wickham. Charlotte, however, notices that Darcy's visit is made soon after his arrival at Rosings and thinks Elizabeth the cause.

Chapter 8

Lady Catherine is now too concerned with her nephews to take much notice of those at the Parsonage. On the occasion when they all meet, Colonel Fitzwilliam takes pleasure in talking to Elizabeth. But Lady Catherine soon wants to know what they are talking about. She must be the centre of everything. She makes an unfeeling invitation for Elizabeth to practise the piano at Rosings, in Mrs Jenkinson's room, out of everybody's way.

Elizabeth captures the attention of both men with her singing, then in the discussion that follows, she upbraids Mr Darcy's manners at the first ball in Hertfordshire when he hardly danced. Darcy defends himself, and there is a new deference in his manner toward Elizabeth. He praises her accomplishment. Elizabeth notes that he responds to Lady Catherine's praise of her daughter without 'any symptom of love'.

COMMENTARY: Darcy has cause to regret the ill-breeding of his aunt. Elizabeth and he continue their repartee where they left off at Netherfield. But Elizabeth fails to notice the new pliancy in his conversation. He does not defend himself against her criticism as strongly as before. This shows he is now in her power. It should also be observed that, despite the prejudice Elizabeth has formed against Darcy through Wickham, she is too lively to be cold toward him. She treats him ironically, but this only deepens her attraction in his eyes. At the same time her charms attract Colonel Fitzwilliam. Elizabeth *is* a very attractive character.

Chapter 9

Elizabeth is alone in the parsonage when Darcy calls. Elizabeth, again direct, raises the subject of Bingley's sudden departure. Darcy will say no more than that Bingley may well have left for good. An apparently ordinary turn in the conversation to the subject of Charlotte's distance from Hertfordshire leads Darcy to make a very forward statement. He says that Elizabeth cannot always have been at Longbourn, meaning that she is superior to her relatives and neighbours. He then draws back and they are almost silent when Charlotte comes in.

Charlotte and Elizabeth both try to understand Darcy's motives. He continues to call often, as does Colonel Fitzwilliam, who is evidently charmed by Elizabeth. But Darcy's withdrawn manner still prevents it being clearly seen that he is in love.

COMMENTARY: Jane Austen is very subtle in her portrayal of the growth of Darcy's feelings. We can see that he is now in love with Elizabeth and working up to his proposal of marriage. But his periods of silence, which occur when he is thinking most deeply, are thought by the others to show his indifference. He makes one sudden intimate remark to Elizabeth and then returns to his formal manner.

Chapter 10

Elizabeth is surprised that she keeps meeting Mr Darcy when on her walks. When he asks her 'odd, unconnected questions', she thinks perhaps he refers to a possible relationship between herself and Colonel Fitzwilliam. But Fitzwilliam has a discussion with her later and mentions that he must marry where there is a fortune. He then tells her that he is joint guardian with Darcy over Miss Darcy, and shows a little anxiety when Elizabeth wonders if she is difficult to manage. The conversation turns to Bingley, and Fitzwilliam tells her that Darcy has recently saved a friend from an imprudent marriage, and he thinks it could have been Bingley.

When alone, Elizabeth becomes very emotional and upset. In her eyes, Darcy's most unforgivable fault is this separation of Bingley and Jane, which has ruined Jane's hopes. She loves her sister very much and knows how little she has deserved such treatment. She is convinced that Darcy's action was motivated by the 'worst kind of pride'. She ends up with a headache and does not go to Rosings for tea with the others.

COMMENTARY: Elizabeth misunderstands Darcy because of his strange manner and her prejudice against him. Otherwise she must see that he is in love with her. Fitzwilliam mentions that Darcy has been delaying their departure. This is evidently because of Elizabeth. He is alarmed by her remark about Miss Darcy in case she knows something of Wickham's attempted seduction. Only he and Darcy know of it as yet. Finally, when she learns about Darcy's part in separating Bingley and Jane, Elizabeth very easily thinks the worst of him: he has ruined the good-natured Jane's happiness merely because of his proud contempt for her low social connections.

Chapter 11

Left alone, Elizabeth reads Jane's uncomplaining letters, revealing all her sadness. She does this 'as if intending to exasperate herself as much as possible against Mr Darcy'. Thus, when Darcy makes his untimely entry, she is in the worst of spirits. Darcy is agitated, speaking in 'a hurried manner' and walking about the room. He then says that after vainly struggling against them, he has come to express his feelings. He loves her. Mistaking her silent astonishment for a good sign, he continues. Now he is 'not more eloquent on the subject of tenderness than pride'. In short, expecting to be accepted, he over-emphasises his struggle against his pride because of her inferior connections. Elizabeth does not even thank him in making her cold reply. Darcy becomes 'pale with anger' and asks what he has done to deserve so uncivil a reply. She answers that he has ruined her sister's happiness, and he does not deny it. She then says he has reduced Wickham to a 'state of poverty'. His pride is roused and he again justifies himself by referring to her inferior relations. She criticises him for not behaving 'in a more gentleman-like manner', and he 'starts' at this. She ends by revealing the dislike she felt towards him from the beginning. He makes a short answer and leaves immediately, leaving Elizabeth to wonder at the content of their interview.

COMMENTARY: This highly dramatic scene is largely self-explanatory. We note the pride of Darcy in making his proposal, and the already prejudiced state in which Elizabeth hears it. She explains everything she has against him. There are several key words and phrases here. Later on in the novel Darcy refers to the justice of Elizabeth's criticism of his 'ungentleman-like manner' at which, we are told, he 'starts'. In revealing all her prejudices to him, Elizabeth gives Darcy a true understanding of her state of mind. On quieter contemplation, both have grounds to re-examine their behaviour up to this point.

Chapter 12

Next day Darcy delivers his letter personally. In it he explains his behaviour in the two points on which Elizabeth had accused him: separating Jane and Bingley, and ruining Wickham's prospects. On the first, he accepts that Bingley was in love with Jane, but he could not see the same feelings in her. Her serene air made him think her not in love. His objection to their marrying was the 'total want of propriety' of her family. But he excluded Jane and Elizabeth from this criticism completely. He had managed to keep Bingley in London by persuading him that Jane did not love him and also he had not told Bingley when she later came to London. Darcy then apologises if he has hurt Jane. The story of Wickham was as follows: Wickham, the son of his father's steward, had been brought up with advantages because of the senior Mr Darcy's regard for his father. But, Darcy's father having died, Wickham asked to exchange the place in the church, which the Darcys had promised him, for a sum of money to help him enter the law. Darcy had paid him this, knowing that Wickham's immoral habits barred him from being a good clergyman. But Wickham asked for the original living back some years later, having not progressed in the law. Darcy refused. That last summer, Wickham had tried to elope with Georgiana Darcy, who was only fifteen. Darcy asks Elizabeth to appeal to Fitzwilliam on the matter if she wants confirmation. His letter ends tenderly.

COMMENTARY: The letter, which begins with cold formality, ends with the words: 'God bless you'. Darcy praises Elizabeth in the letter and presents his reasons and the relevant details very fairly. It shows that his regard for her has not lessened, and is a turning point in his conquering of his pride.

Chapter 13

Elizabeth reads at first 'with a strong prejudice against everything he might say', but reads Darcy's account a second and a third time. At first trying to prove it false, she is brought to see the justice of his story about Wickham. Wickham's remarks to her in Meryton had been indiscreet, and he did not live up to his boast that he would not avoid Darcy. She realises that she has misjudged Darcy and she has been prejudiced against him. Wickham, in comparison, had behaved very badly, but she had been too ready to judge in his favour. For example, she had defended his behaviour toward Miss King. She is ashamed and sees she has been 'blind, partial, prejudiced, absurd', and the cause of it was her own vanity. Even Darcy's explanations about Jane were understandable. Charlotte also had thought Jane looked too serene to be in love. The behaviour of her family had really caused Jane all her unhappiness.

With these feelings, Elizabeth returns to the Parsonage to find Darcy and Fitzwilliam have already left their farewells.

COMMENTARY: Some critics have said that Elizabeth's change of heart is too quick to be believed. But Darcy's arguments are logical. Wickham's guilt is indeed obvious, and Jane Austen has prepared her readers for Darcy's account of the relationship between Bingley and Jane by earlier events in the novel. We remember how Charlotte had suggested at the ball that Jane ought to encourage Bingley more. On other occasions as well, the author has given evidence of Jane's calm outward appearance which hid the fact that she was really in love. Yet despite all these good reasons, perhaps it is just the suddenness of Elizabeth's change of attitude toward Darcy which could be criticised.

Chapter 14

Elizabeth dines again at Rosings but has to report her impending departure. Still pondering Darcy's letter, she feels compassion, respect, and gratitude towards him. The awareness that her family had spoilt Jane's chances returns when she thinks of going home. Her father had failed to show authority, her mother knew nothing of right or wrong, and Lydia and Catherine were 'ignorant, idle and vain'.

COMMENTARY: Elizabeth's reflections show the growth in her understanding. She is now to leave her 'prejudice' behind her, and move toward a position where she can fully appreciate Darcy.

Chapter 15

Mr Collins once more tries to make Elizabeth regret what Charlotte has gained. She again can only feel sorry for her friend when she leaves. She meets Jane again in London.

COMMENTARY: Charlotte has chosen her lot with Collins 'with her eyes open'. Elizabeth's visit has only confirmed her belief that marriage without affection, for social position alone, is undesirable and imprudent.

Chapter 16

It is now May (Elizabeth arrived at Hunsford in March). Returning to Longbourn, Elizabeth and Jane meet Kitty and Lydia. There is news that Wickham's regiment is leaving Meryton for Brighton, and that Miss King has left the area. Lydia jokes and behaves irresponsibly till they reach home. Mr Bennet is most glad to see Elizabeth again. Elizabeth attempts to keep her younger sisters in order and is against Lydia's plea that they should all go to Brighton.

COMMENTARY: This chapter is notable for its fuller development of Lydia's character. She is irresponsible in buying a useless bonnet, and tells many jokes. Jane Austen is preparing us for her elopement. Already the scheme of going to Brighton has been put forward.

Chapter 17

Elizabeth tells Jane of Darcy's proposal and the details of his letter, except what concerns her and Bingley. Jane finds it difficult to believe Wickham so bad, especially considering his attractive manners, but since he is leaving they decide not to tell the truth about him. Jane is still unhappy without Bingley. Mrs Bennet has the melancholy mind of an old woman, believing Jane will die, and doubting the Collinses' marriage will last, though at the same time continuing to argue the injustice of their inheriting Longbourn.

COMMENTARY: The decision that Elizabeth and Jane make not to expose Wickham's history to anyone else is crucial in the development of the plot.

Chapter 18

Mrs Bennet and the youngest daughters wish to go to Brighton, but Mr Bennet will not allow it. Elizabeth remembers Darcy's objections and again feels shame for her family. Lydia is invited to Brighton by her friend, the newly-married Mrs Forster. Kitty is cross and jealous. Elizabeth points out to her father the dangers of allowing Lydia to go. He argues that having no money she will be no prey to anyone, and that she will see her own unimportance. Elizabeth pleads in vain for the family's dignity.

Wickham comes with the officers to dine at Longbourn. Elizabeth tells him she saw Darcy and Fitzwilliam at Rosings, and that now she better appreciates Darcy's qualities. Wickham is hypocritical enough to praise Darcy ironically for adopting a better 'appearance', and repeats his charge that Darcy is proud.

COMMENTARY: Mr Bennet's lack of parental authority is confirmed. His sarcasm about Lydia scaring off Elizabeth's lovers and needing to display herself in a public place is too ironically correct to be humorous.

Elizabeth now sees Wickham correctly. Jane Austen uses the word 'appearance' twice—when Wickham charges Darcy with the appearance of doing what is right, and when Wickham appears to be his usual cheerful self, although injured by knowing Elizabeth no longer believes him.

Chapter 19

We learn the background of the Bennets' marriage. Mr Bennet was 'captivated by youth and beauty' and married a woman without intelligence. Affection had worn off and Mr Bennet turned to his library for consolation. He takes pleasure in laughing at his wife's 'ignorance and folly'. At this time, Elizabeth has never been more conscious of the mistake of such a marriage.

Elizabeth's journey to the Lake District has to be shortened to only as far as Derbyshire because of Mr Gardiner. Mrs Gardiner leaves her children at Longbourn. When they reach Derbyshire she suggests a visit to Darcy's residence, Pemberley. Elizabeth only consents to go on hearing that Darcy is away.

COMMENTARY: Jane Austen gently satirises Mr Bennet's position—he is seen as 'the true philosopher' making the best of his lot. Elizabeth's view is closer to the truth. Having seen her parents' marriage, and the Collinses' marriage, she has good examples of how not to marry. Marriage for money alone, or for passion alone, is not good.

Volume 3: Chapter 1

The next day they visit Pemberley. It stands on rising ground amongst scenery laid out with good taste. The housekeeper shows them around the well-proportioned, handsome house. Elizabeth cannot help thinking how she might have been mistress of it all, as Darcy's wife, but recollects that Darcy's pride would have barred her uncle and aunt from seeing her there. The housekeeper tells her that Darcy will return the next day. Seeing Elizabeth attracted to Wickham's portrait, she tells her 'he has turned out very wild'. The Gardiners encourage the housekeeper to speak freely of Darcy and we learn that he has never spoken a cross word to her. He was a good-natured child, and now he is generous to his tenants and servants. But he is quiet by nature. He is an excellent brother to his sister. Mrs Gardiner is surprised, knowing Darcy only from Wickham's report. But Elizabeth, viewing Darcy's portrait, is moved to a new esteem of his character and feels gratitude toward him.

Leaving the house, they suddenly meet Darcy. Both he and Elizabeth are very embarrassed. She feels the impropriety of them being there. Though not at ease, he speaks to her with marked courtesy. When he leaves, the contrast between his manner now, and when she last saw him, strikes her forcibly.

Darcy meets them again in the park (which is beyond the near precints of the house). She introduces her relatives, and he is evidently surprised, especially as her uncle talks to him with taste and intelligence. Darcy invites him to come to fish there. As they walk back to the house, Elizabeth and Darcy get further ahead. Elizabeth explains she had expected him not to be at home. He invites her to meet his sister.

In their carriage, Mr and Mrs Gardiner praise Darcy, although Mrs Gardiner still cannot get Wickham's story out of her mind.

COMMENTARY: The chance coincidence of Elizabeth meeting Darcy at Pemberley is the only event in the book which seems especially contrived by the author. It brings them both together again. Both have changed. The change in Darcy's behaviour toward Elizabeth is not so surprising when it comes after his housekeeper's high praise of him. This is the first time that we, like Elizabeth, hear of another side to his character. 'That he was not a good-tempered man, had been her firmest opinion', and when we recall his behaviour at the balls and other occasions, we can see that this opinion is not unjustified. But now we learn of the Darcy that those who know him best can see. Above all, his behaviour toward Elizabeth is now quite free of pride. He is trying to behave 'in a more gentleman-like manner'.

Chapter 2

Next day, Darcy brings his sister to see Elizabeth. His behaviour makes the Gardiners suspect he is attracted to their niece. Georgiana Darcy, rumoured to be proud, is really only shy. Then Bingley appears and inquires about her family. Everyone gets on well together. Elizabeth sees that Bingley and Miss Darcy are not in love as Miss Bingley had suggested. She notes some regret in Bingley when he refers to his departure from Netherfield. Darcy wishes to please as never before. Elizabeth and her relatives are invited to dine at Pemberley. Enquiries in the district add to Wickham's bad name. Elizabeth is left to reflect on the good actions of Darcy, and to feel gratitude to him for not resenting her refusal of marriage.

COMMENTARY: The rumour and half-truths that have stained the reputation of Darcy and his sister fall away. Bingley still loves Jane. The way seems open for the two men to renew their proposals in much improved circumstances.

Chapter 3

Mrs Gardiner and Elizabeth visit Georgiana. The Bingley sisters are also present. Conversation is strained because of Georgiana's shyness and the Bingleys' rudeness. When Darcy comes in, Miss Bingley watches him for signs of regard for Elizabeth. She attempts to crush a relationship developing between Miss Darcy and Elizabeth by raising the subject of Wickham. Her plan misfires, for Georgiana and Darcy are more embarrassed than Elizabeth. Miss Bingley is unaware of Wickham's behaviour toward Miss Darcy. Elizabeth's 'collected behaviour' restores everyone's nerves. When she leaves for her carriage, Miss Bingley conducts a campaign of criticism against Elizabeth that only ends with her challenging Darcy directly. She recalls a sharp remark that Darcy had once made about her beauty. Darcy replies that now he thinks the opposite.

COMMENTARY: Jane Austen excels in portraying the selfishness and pettiness of short-sighted people. The character of Miss Bingley is a fine study in female hypocrisy, back-biting and jealousy. Her direct remark to Darcy, although it can only hurt herself, shows Jane Austen's deep penetration of human behaviour: 'this was not the best method of recommending herself; but angry people are not always wise'. The judgement is objective and unbiased.

Chapter 4

Two letters arrive from Jane. The first contains news that Lydia and Wickham have eloped from Brighton, but is hopeful they intend to marry. The second informs Elizabeth that no such marriage is likely to have taken place, since Lydia and Wickham seem not to have gone to Gretna Green in Scotland, where quick marriage ceremonies were performed. Mr Bennet is to leave for London where it is believed the couple have gone.

Elizabeth is greatly shaken by the news. Darcy comes in just as she is about to get up. A servant is sent to her uncle, while she tells Darcy. She reproaches herself for not having revealed Wickham's character. If she had, she believes this would never have happened. She thinks she sees in Darcy's silence a decline in his estimation of her. Once more, she feels, her family have ruined all her chances, at the moment when she now realises that 'she could have loved' Darcy.

When Darcy leaves, Elizabeth looks back on the time in Derbyshire with regret. Thinking of Lydia and Wickham, she cannot believe they could have married. Wickham would gain nothing from it. Elizabeth and the Gardiners then set out for Longbourn.

COMMENTARY: Jane Austen often uses the literary technique of creating a last, serious obstacle, before the calm, favourable endings of her books. This is what the elopment stands for in the plot. It clarifies Elizabeth's love for Darcy, but at the same time wakens her, and our, anxiety that they can not now be fulfilled. The happy prospects which had been built up in Derbyshire seem now to be crushed, 'and never had she so honestly felt that she could have loved him, as now, when all love must be vain'.

Chapter 5

Mr and Mrs Gardiner brighten Elizabeth's spirits for a short while by giving reasons to hope that Wickham would marry Lydia. But Elizabeth soon recalls, in the frivolous nature of Lydia and the unprincipled character of Wickham, the fallacy of these hopes. She tells them some of the truth about Wickham's past behaviour.

They reach Longbourn and find that Jane is still keeping up her hopes, whilst Mrs Bennet, in the absence of her husband, is in a fit of depression. Mary Bennet makes high moral observations which are of no use at all. Mr Gardiner goes to London.

Jane tells Elizabeth more details. Colonel Forster did not believe Wickham intended to marry Lydia when they eloped, having heard in the regiment things to alter his original good opinion of Wickham. A letter from Lydia to Mrs Forster shows her complete lack of responsibility in the reasons she gives for eloping. Jane explains how Mrs Bennet had been hysterical at first.

COMMENTARY: We see the Bennet family in complete disarray. Mr Bennet has left to try to find the couple, but has no success. Mrs Bennet blames everyone but herself, and believes Mr Bennet will be killed in a duel with Wickham. Mary Bennet only underlines the ineptitude of the family. Only Jane and Elizabeth properly understand the situation. Elizabeth's criticism of her family is seen to be completely true. Lydia's letter makes this very plain.

Chapter 6

Mrs Philips comes with black stories about Wickham's bad character. Everybody's opinion about him is now completely reversed. Those left at Longbourn anxiously await news. A letter comes from Mr Collins saying that Lydia's death would have been better than what she has done, and advising Mr Bennet to renounce her. He scarcely conceals his relief that he had not married Elizabeth, and adds that the girls' marriage prospects would now be very dim.

Wickham's debts in Brighton are reported. Mr Bennet returns, although Mrs Bennet now wishes him to remain in London to fight Wickham and make him marry Lydia. Mr Bennet is now very philosophical, and acknowledges his own guilt. But this, and his threat to Kitty to keep her almost confined to the house, are not really meant seriously.

COMMENTARY: The characters of Mrs Bennet, Collins, and Mr Bennet, are all brought out in their folly. Collins, especially, writes a letter which is outrageously selfish and hypocritical. Mrs Bennet is wholly inconsistent, and Mr Bennet still, at heart, has no power over his family.

Chapter 7

Mr Bennet receives news from Mr Gardiner that Lydia and Wickham have been found unmarried, but that a marriage settlement has been arranged. Elizabeth and Mr Bennet both realise that Wickham has been offered a substantial sum of money and conclude it must be Mr Gardiner's doing. Elizabeth reflects on the impropriety of such a marriage, but realises there is no alternative. Jane's hopes, however, are more optimistic.

When Mrs Bennet hears the news she changes completely in mood. All the past seems to be forgotten as she rejoices in the thought of having a daughter married at sixteen, and of what wedding clothes Lydia shall wear. She is not thankful to Mr Gardiner, for she thinks it is his natural duty to help them. Elizabeth is sick of her mother's folly and retires.

COMMENTARY: Lydia's marriage is arranged under the most unhopeful circumstances. Elizabeth realises it has been badly arranged just as she had thought Charlotte's marriage had been. Jane's reaction shows her naïve understanding, and Mrs Bennet's, her lack of any understanding at all.

Chapter 8

Jane Austen gives the financial background to Lydia's marriage, explaining how it is not disadvantageous to Mr Bennet's pocket. Mr Bennet at first refuses to allow the married couple to come to Longbourn, or to pay for wedding clothes. Elizabeth believes that Darcy would not want to marry into a family into which Wickham was also married. This makes her think all the more how well-suited to marry she and Darcy would have been. In comparison, Lydia and Wickham, brought together by passion alone, must be quite unsuited.

All but Mrs Bennet are relieved that Wickham will go to another regiment in the north of England, far away from Longbourn.

COMMENTARY: Jane Austen shows that financial considerations were very significant when it came to marriage in her world. Having disapproved of Charlotte's very worldly marriage, Elizabeth is, however, just as critical of a marriage founded solely on passion. But a marriage between her and Darcy would be a good one because their characters would complement each other. Also, Darcy has a very good fortune.

Chapter 9

Lydia and Wickham do come to Longbourn. Both are unchanged and not at all sorry for their behaviour. Lydia is still 'untamed, unabashed, wild, noisy and fearless'. Several things in her behaviour show her lack of taste. She says: 'When I went away, I am sure I had no more idea of being married till I came back again! Though I thought it would be very good fun if I was.' This shows she has no sense of the efforts made by others to compel Wickham to marry her. Then she says to Jane, the eldest sister, that she must now be lower in rank to herself because she is a married woman.

Elizabeth is angry at all this. She sees that Wickham does not love Lydia, but merely eloped with her because of the momentary circumstances. Lydia insists on giving an account of her wedding day. She says her aunt was trying to preach a sermon to her, but she was only concerned about how Wickham would dress for the ceremony. By accident she mentions that Darcy was present. She tells her sisters it was supposed to be a secret. Elizabeth is, of course, very anxious to know why, and writes to Mrs Gardiner.

COMMENTARY: Lydia's attitude to marriage is very shallow indeed. Later we learn that when Darcy found her she was living in London with Wickham with no thought of marrying him. Her comments are full of unconscious irony, as when she says her sisters should go to Brighton, for that is the place to get husbands. She dotes over Wickham in complete ignorance of his true character.

Chapter 10

Mrs Gardiner's letter tells the part Darcy had played in arranging the marriage. He found Wickham through Mrs Younge, the woman who had been Miss Darcy's governess and who had helped Wickham in his plans to elope with her. Darcy persuaded Wickham to marry Lydia by paying his debts and giving him a cash settlement. Lydia had refused to leave Wickham, although not married to him. Darcy and Mr Gardiner then arranged the wedding. Darcy had behaved very generously, explaining as his motive his wish to make amends for not exposing

Wickham's bad character. But Mrs Gardiner sees that he really did it for the sake of Elizabeth. She ends by hinting that, were they to marry, Elizabeth could supply Darcy with the one quality he lacked—'liveliness'.

Although in 'a flutter of spirits' as a result of this news, Elizabeth still cannot be sure that Darcy did do all this for her sake. She feels the obligation her family owe to Darcy and groans at her past behaviour toward him: 'For herself she was humbled, but she was proud of him'.

Wickham interrupts Elizabeth's thoughts. They discuss his past in such a way that Wickham at last realises Elizabeth knows his whole story.

COMMENTARY: From Mrs Gardiner's letter we learn of Darcy's behaviour since Elizabeth and he parted in Derbyshire. Far from letting the elopement stop his wish to marry Elizabeth, he takes much trouble and expense to uphold the outward respectability of her family. He had to deal with Wickham, the man his pride detested most. Elizabeth is humbly aware of his generosity and regrets her past sharp words to him. She totally understands the obligation her family owe him, but still cannot be sure that he wants to marry her.

The scene with Wickham is a masterpiece of innuendo and irony, and shows us Wickham subtly, but definitely exposed.

Chapter 11

The opening sentence is ironic; Wickham never brings up the subject again but he retains his old superficial charm when the time comes for goodbyes. Mr Bennet sarcastically praises Wickham's manners. Mrs Bennet is upset to see Lydia go, but soon forgets when she leaves, for Bingley is going to return to Netherfield.

Jane again controls her feelings. But Mrs Bennet renews her schemes, telling Mr Bennet he must call on Bingley when he comes.

Bingley visits Longbourn with Darcy soon after his arrival. Both sisters are uncomfortable. Elizabeth is astonished at Darcy's coming. She watches him, but he is mostly silent and looks at the ground. She is very conscious of the unrevealed obligation her family owe him, and is ashamed when Mrs Bennet speaks at length about Lydia's marriage, showing no sense of shame herself. She feels that the same obstacle as before—her mother's stupidity—will bring the same result. But Bingley begins to talk with Jane and ends by accepting Mrs Bennet's invitation to dine at Longbourn.

COMMENTARY: The storm of Lydia's elopement is now over. Although Elizabeth goes through misery because of her mother, this time the way is prepared for a happy ending. Jane Austen reminds us that a year has passed since the opening of the story. To underline this, Mr and Mrs Bennet seem to begin the same argument as they had done at the beginning: whether Mr Bennet should visit Mr Bingley. But this time Bingley and Darcy take the initiative, although Darcy has still to overcome his shyness. Darcy has given Bingley his approval to court Jane.

Chapter 12

Both sisters are nervous about their lovers. When the men come to dinner, Bingley sits by Jane and they renew their intimacy. Mr Darcy sits far away from Elizabeth, next to Mrs Bennet, who hardly hides her dislike. For Jane the evening is a great success, but Darcy and Elizabeth hardly speak to each other owing to his reserve and her mother's organisation. Jane is still cautious about admitting that she loves Bingley.

COMMENTARY: While the courtship of Bingley and Jane is heading to its favourable conclusion, Darcy and Elizabeth still have to overcome their reticence and doubts.

Chapter 13

Mrs Bennet schemes to get Bingley and Jane alone by pretending she needs her other daughters elsewhere. Bingley behaves with 'ease and cheerfulness', and overlooks Mrs Bennet's bad taste. Darcy has gone to London, and Bingley goes shooting with Mr Bennet. That evening Elizabeth mistakenly interrupts a love scene between Jane and Bingley. Bingley goes to get Mr Bennet's permission and Jane reveals their engagement. Elizabeth believes they will be happy because of Jane's understanding and excellent disposition, and their similarity in taste. Mr Bennet congratulates Jane, saying their easy-going characters will mean the servants will always cheat them. Both Jane and Bingley make Elizabeth the confidant of their happiness. Jane tells her that Bingley had left Netherfield still loving her but had stayed away because he thought she was indifferent to him.

Mrs Bennet soon spreads the news.

COMMENTARY: Jane Austen reveals her views on the best grounds for marriage through Elizabeth's thoughts. She says that 'in spite of being a lover', Bingley's hopes of happiness were 'rationally founded' because of Jane's 'excellent understanding' and their similar feelings and taste. We see that Jane Austen is very aware that to be 'in love' is not enough; very often lovers' feelings are mistaken. But when characters are suitably matched, and there is love (and also, in Jane and Bingley's case, plenty of money) then there is a good chance of success in marriage.

Chapter 14

Lady Catherine de Bourgh makes a surprise visit to Longbourn. She speaks to Elizabeth alone in the garden. She is 'now more than usually insolent and disagreeable'. The reason is that she has heard a report that Elizabeth is to marry Darcy, her nephew. She accuses Elizabeth of spreading this report. Elizabeth refuses to answer Lady Catherine's questions. Lady Catherine claims that Darcy is engaged to her daughter: the match had long been desired by both families and will not now be prevented 'by a young woman of inferior birth, of no importance in the world'. Elizabeth insists that she and Darcy have the right to make their own choice. Lady Catherine emphasises Elizabeth's lower social rank and commands her to promise that she will not become engaged to Darcy. Elizabeth refuses and says she has no intention of being influenced by Lady Catherine. Her own affairs are no business of Lady Catherine. When Lady Catherine brings up the subject of Lydia's 'patched-up' marriage, Elizabeth says she has no more to say.

COMMENTARY: Lady Catherine's attempt to frighten Elizabeth with her rank has no effect. Elizabeth refuses to be bullied, and recognising the weaknesses in Lady Catherine's position, counter-attacks with intelligent answers. Lady Catherine leaves defeated. We later learn that she goes to Darcy to try to persuade him against the engagement. Her attempts, however, only make Darcy realise Elizabeth will marry him, so Lady Catherine achieves exactly the opposite of her intention.

Chapter 15

Elizabeth suffers 'discomposure of spirits' after this argument. She reasons that the Lucases must have spread the rumour, and Mr Collins has reported it to Lady Catherine. She fears that Lady Catherine will see Darcy and persuade him against marrying her.

Mr Bennet calls Elizabeth into the library and reads her a letter in which Collins congratulates Mr Bennet on a marriage between Darcy and Elizabeth, at the same time advising against it, and reporting Lady Catherine's displeasure. He then criticises Mr Bennet for allowing Lydia to visit Longbourn after her behaviour. Mr Bennet is very amused by the whole letter, but considers the prospect of Elizabeth marrying Darcy to be particularly ridiculous. Elizabeth is forced to laugh, though inwardly very hurt.

COMMENTARY: Elizabeth has to undergo more suffering, first, because she is still unsure of Darcy's feelings, and, secondly, because of her father's unconscious callousness. Mr Collins's letter again shows Jane Austen's love of irony. Collins sees the obvious materialistic advantages of the match for the Bennets, is sure they will accept it, but advises them against it. His remarks about Lydia being forgiven, but never again mentioned, are criticised by Mr Bennet as unchristian.

Chapter 16

Darcy comes with Bingley to Longbourn. The four lovers set out for a walk, also with Kitty. Bingley and Jane separate from the others and Kitty leaves Darcy and Elizabeth alone a little further on. Elizabeth manages to express feelings of gratitude to Darcy for his behaviour over Lydia. He tells her it was meant to be kept secret, and that he did it for herself alone. He then says briefly that his feelings are still the same. Elizabeth explains the alteration in her feelings and intimates that she accepts his proposal (Jane Austen, however, merely states this briefly without giving any dialogue). Both wish to apologise for their past conduct. Darcy, especially, emphasises the effect her words 'had you behaved in a more gentleman-like manner' had had upon him. He admits he has been proud since his childhood, but Elizabeth has humbled him. Elizabeth, in turn, tells how she began to change after reading Darcy's letter. Darcy ends by telling how he had admitted his mistake about Jane to Bingley, and this had caused Bingley to renew his suit. Elizabeth resists a joke at Darcy's expense about how pliable Bingley is as a friend.

COMMENTARY: This chapter attempts to explain the changes that have been going on in Darcy throughout the novel. Up until now, we have only seen him through the eyes of Elizabeth and the report of others. Now, for the first time, we see his point of view. In particular, he stresses how his love for Elizabeth finally humbled his pride. We may remember that a little earlier Elizabeth had been so described: 'for herself she was humbled; but she was proud of him'. Thus both have changed and learnt more about themselves during the novel.

Chapter 17

Elizabeth tells Jane first and is dismayed that even she is shocked by the news. She and Bingley had thought it impossible. But she soon wishes Elizabeth happiness and the complete story is unfolded to her, including Darcy's helping Lydia.

Mrs Bennet still describes Mr Darcy as 'disagreeable'. She sends Elizabeth out to walk with him so Jane and Bingley can be together, apologising that Elizabeth must walk with 'that disagreeable man' alone.

In the evening Darcy goes to get Mr Bennet's permission. When Mr Bennet has Elizabeth in his library he asks her if she knows what she is doing. Mr Bennet still considers Darcy proud and unpleasant. He wants Elizabeth to marry a man she can respect, not, he implies, a person lower than herself, like his own wife. Elizabeth insists on her true love for Darcy and tells Mr Bennet that Darcy had helped Lydia. Mr Bennet sarcastically remarks that now he will not have to pay any money because Darcy would never accept it. He ends by saying that if anyone comes for Mary or Kitty he is ready to see them.

Mrs Bennet's reaction is to change her opinion of Darcy very rapidly. Now he is: 'Such a charming man!—so handsome! so tall!' Then she thinks of all the material benefits Elizabeth will have, and says she must have a special marriage licence to speed the marriage.

COMMENTARY: For the first time, Mr Bennet shows some concern about his daughters, Elizabeth being his favourite. He does not want her to be as unhappy in marriage as he has been. Mrs Bennet, on the other hand, cares only that another daughter is to be married, and to the richest husband of all. ' 'Tis as good as a Lord!' she says.

Chapter 18

Darcy gives his reasons for loving Elizabeth: her liveliness of mind; her affectionate nature, as seen in her love toward Jane; and (though this is not actually stated) her beauty. He explains that on the occasions she thought him indifferent, his quietness was due to his reserve and shyness. His feelings were so strong he was unable to talk about them at the time. He confirms that Lady Catherine's intervention had encouraged him to ask Elizabeth a second time.

Elizabeth writes to Mrs Gardiner in a gay mood, announcing the engagement. Mr Bennet writes to Collins advising him to console Lady Catherine but support Darcy who has more advantages to give.

Miss Bingley writes her hypocritical congratulations to Jane. Miss Darcy is sincerely pleased with Darcy's fiancée. Charlotte flees from Kent because of Lady Catherine's anger at the news of Darcy's engagement.

COMMENTARY: Once more we get a fuller picture of Darcy's past behaviour. We learn he is a man of reserve and deep feelings, and that others have mistaken this for pride. Elizabeth continues to make humorous remarks and thus sets the pattern for their future together. Darcy suffers her vulgar relatives while he has to.

Chapter 19

The author ties up all the ends of her story. Bingley and Jane leave Netherfield after a year and live thirty miles from Pemberley. Kitty has the chance to improve in the good society provided by her married sisters. Lydia receives money from Elizabeth and Darcy does help Wickham in his career. Miss Darcy and Elizabeth grow to love each other, and Georgiana sees her brother treated playfully by his wife. Both Mr Bennet and the Gardiners make frequent visits, and even Lady Catherine is eventually brought to visit Pemberley as well.

COMMENTARY: The novel reaches a favourable ending after the trials and difficulties it has portrayed. The future of each of the characters seems consistent with what we would expect from the knowledge we have of them.

Part 3

Commentary

The characters

Elizabeth Bennet

Elizabeth is her father's favourite daughter, having inherited his wit and intelligence. 'Lizzy has something more of quickness than her sisters', he says. She has a healthy sense of humour, even to the point of joking about Mr Darcy's rude behaviour toward herself at the ball. We are told that 'she had a lively, playful disposition, which delighted in anything ridiculous'. She has much spirit, matching Mr Darcy in intricate and subtle arguments, and standing up to Lady Catherine de Bourgh. She is even impulsive, as when she walks three miles through dirty fields to come to her sick sister at Netherfield. This also shows her affectionate nature, which is one reason Darcy gives for loving her. Although she becomes very prejudiced against Darcy, her behaviour only increases his admiration, for: 'there was a mixture of sweetness and archness in her manner which made it difficult for her to affront anybody'. Not only Mr Bennet and Darcy, but also Sir William Lucas, Colonel Fitzwilliam, and, of course, Wickham, admire her.

But Elizabeth, for all her intelligence and usual penetration, makes bad mistakes of judgement. She lets Wickham's manners and appearance bias her against Darcy. She allows her own pride to prejudice herself against him. She is inconsistent in disapproving Charlotte Lucas's worldly marriage, but supporting Wickham in his pursuit of an heiress (though even this shows her lack of jealousy and serious vanity). Otherwise, she sees the bad-breeding of her younger sisters and the folly of her mother. Her advice to her father against Lydia going to Brighton is mature and realistic. When she falls in love with Darcy, she does so having first felt respect and gratitude toward him. Although not anxious by nature, her periods of deepest disquiet are over Jane's unhappiness and her own uncertainty over Darcy.

Elizabeth has originality, especially in her liveliness, which makes her an interesting character. In doing the unexpected, but at the same time remaining sensible, she is a more life-like heroine than the conventional heroine of sentimental novels.

Appearance: although not so obvious a beauty as her sister Jane, it is her eyes and expression which captivate Darcy.

Social position: Elizabeth is the Bennets' second daughter, twenty years old, but without any fortune to attract worldly suitors.

Fitzwilliam Darcy

Darcy comes to Netherfield as Bingley's friend. He is aloof and superior in his behaviour toward their new acquaintances. He only dances with Bingley's sisters at the first ball, and he slights Elizabeth. Even Jane, he thinks, 'smiled too much'. His manners are proud, and his speech measured and formal. He has a fine library at Pemberley and, according to Bingley, 'he studies too much for words of four syllables' when writing letters. The vulgarity of the Bennet family soon offends him.

However, Elizabeth attracts him against his will. To her, he tries to open out and explain his character, but she is at first indifferent, and then prejudiced against him. He admits his temper is 'too little yielding'; but retains his pride which, he says, has always kept him from showing the folly and vanity of other people. Yet behind his reserve and fastidiousness there are genuine qualities. He is generous to his servants, his tenants, and most affectionate to his sister. He knows the meaning of discretion, in, for instance, his dealings with Wickham, which Elizabeth later acknowledges are very fair. He is, in fact, a good man who has been made stiff and proud by his upbringing. It is Elizabeth who is able to humble him, although their courtship is a troubled one owing to their mutual failings. Darcy, as a lover, is deeply in love, but shy and embarrassed. His strong feelings prevent him being a romantic, sentimental lover. Elizabeth realises that Wickham, who seems to fit that role, is totally inferior to Darcy.

Appearance: Darcy is a 'fine, tall person' with 'handsome features' and 'noble mien'.

Social position: he has an income of £10,000 a year, a large, elegant country house and estate, and comes from a long established family on the verge of the aristocracy.

Jane Bennet

Jane is the eldest and most beautiful of the Bennet sisters. She is the natural choice of Bingley as partner at the Meryton ball. She never thinks ill of anybody, and has, in addition to her warm sympathetic feelings, an outward composure and easy manner. She 'united with great strength of feeling, composure of temper and a uniform cheerfulness of manner, which would guard her from the suspicious or the impertinent'. She is not capable of guile, of 'helping on' Bingley, as Charlotte Lucas advises. She suffers patiently, even, Elizabeth feels, 'angelically'.

But Jane's judgement is faulty. She takes a long time to see Miss Bingley's hypocrisy; she is no more able to see what Wickham is really like than anyone else. She refuses to believe that he could live with Lydia without marrying her, and still imagines their marriage may be a happy one after all. She also believes Charlotte and Collins may be happy. Her own marriage to Bingley would have been accomplished with ease were it not for the disadvantage of her family, and Darcy's influence over Bingley. As it eventually turns out, Elizabeth sees they were meant for each other and nothing could be more natural than their marriage.

Appearance: Jane's beauty is the first thing we learn about her. It gains her an eligible husband despite her lack of fortune.

Social position: at twenty-two, Jane is the daughter Mrs Bennet most hopes to get married. She has the advantage of beauty, but has no wealth.

Charles Bingley

Bingley is a straightforward, genial person. He is no snob, like his sisters, but gentleman-like and prepared to fit in with most people. He is not seriously put off by Jane's relatives. He is, however, a little too easily influenced. He does not trust his own feelings, but allows others to separate Jane and himself. But once Darcy removes his objection, Bingley proposes to Jane without the slow caution of his friend.

Appearance: 'He was quite young, wonderfully handsome, extremely agreeable . . .' in the eyes of his female neighbours. 'He had a pleasant countenance, and easy, unaffected manners.'

Social position: Bingley has an income of between £4,000 and £5,000 a year. He has not yet bought an estate. Unlike Darcy, he comes from the new rich—those who have made money in trade and risen socially.

Mr Bennet

Mr Bennet is an intelligent man, and a 'gentleman' by birth, which means he has inherited property. But having made an unwise marriage with a woman of low intelligence, he retreats into his library. When he is with his family, he takes pleasure in ridiculing his ignorant wife and his daughters. He calls his daughters 'silly and ignorant like other girls'. With no one to understand him, except Elizabeth, he takes up the isolated position of 'a philosopher'. But his sarcasm does not justify his neglect of his daughters. He fails to discipline them, allowing, instead, their mother to encourage their ignorance and vanity.

Mr Bennet often makes penetrating remarks, and is the source of much of Jane Austen's choicest irony. For all his faults, he is a likeable man. But he is almost as guilty as Mrs Bennet for the sufferings of Jane and Elizabeth, and the unsuitable marriage Lydia makes, and he is a character who does not change by the end of the novel. However, he gains happiness through Elizabeth's marriage, as after it he often visits Pemberley. He and his daughter are much alike in their wit, humour and intelligence.

Social position: a gentleman through his ownership of the Longbourn estate, he has, however, married beneath himself socially, and is unable to provide his daughters with a dowry. Added to this, his estate is entailed to the male line and he has no son to inherit it.

Mrs Bennet

'She was a woman of mean understanding, little information, and uncertain temper. When she was discontented she fancied herself nervous. The business of her life was to get her daughters married, its solace was visiting and news.' In this description of her chief comic character, Jane Austen summarises what we learn of Mrs Bennet throughout the book. She is jealous of her neighbours, except when she can triumph over them. Her obsession with her daughters is really, at heart, a selfish one, for she was beautiful herself once, and now she relives her vanity through them, especially through Jane and Lydia. She backbites (that is, criticises someone unfairly when they are not present) and wishes always to have her own way. Her schemes to marry off her daughters show womanly wiles, but they are carried out with exaggeration and no subtlety. Although an attorney's daughter, she cannot understand the meaning of the estate being entailed. She plagues Jane with her indiscreet attempts to further the match with Bingley.

When things go wrong, Mrs Bennet becomes irritable and complains of her nerves. Lydia's elopement at first sends her into a fit of hysteria. But when she hears that she will be married, she forgets all moral considerations. She is quite unthankful toward Mr Gardiner, who all believe has bought off Wickham. But her biggest change of face comes with Darcy. From being 'disagreeable' and 'hateful', he is suddenly 'charming', when he becomes engaged to Elizabeth. Petty and materialistic though she is, Mrs Bennet is yet a rich object of Jane Austen's satire and comedy. As there is no hope of reforming her character, like Mr Bennet, we come to enjoy laughing at her ridiculous behaviour.

Mr Collins

The personality of Collins is revealed as much in his letters as in his actual behaviour. The letter announcing his intended visit to Longbourn is long and formal, and when he arrives he turns out to be pompous and long-winded in his speeches. In fact, he carries his formality and affected humility to the point of ridiculousness. He says he comes 'prepared to admire' the Bennet girls, and his courtship of Elizabeth, ending in the proposal of marriage (which is hyperbolical, carried to absurd conclusion) is all the more humorous because he is completely unaware of anyone's feelings but his own. Even Collins's own feelings are unstable—he turns from Jane, to Elizabeth, to Charlotte in far too rapid succession.

Collins, as Mr Bennet understands at once, is 'absurd'. He is not well-educated, but has adopted 'a mixture of pride and obsequiousness, of self-importance and humility'. His perception does not go beyond outward formalities and social standards. He praises Lady Catherine excessively because she is his patroness and his social superior. He can only appreciate anything in so far as its cost or its outward grandeur is evident. He especially points out to his visitors the number of trees at Rosings and the number and cost of the windows.

Collins is a very worldly clergyman, and he is mainly concerned with visiting his patroness and carrying out the prescribed rituals of the Church. That he has no deeper Christian feeling is shown by his advice to Mr Bennet that Lydia be forgiven for her behaviour with Wickham, but never spoken to again.

George Wickham

Wickham's character and appearance must be discussed together: 'His appearance was greatly in his favour; he had all the best part of beauty, a fine countenance, a good figure, a very pleasing address.' These outward advantages he uses so well that he deceives everyone. He bends the facts with subtlety to give them a false appearance, and sometimes he tells a direct lie. However, because he says everything so well he is able to get away with his deception: 'his manners recommended him to everybody. Whatever he said, was said well; and whatever he did, done gracefully'. He is the exact opposite of Darcy. Elizabeth, at first deceived by his appearance, realises the truth of the matter when she says: 'one has got all the good qualities, and the other all the appearance of it'.

Wickham's seduction of Lydia follows his attempted seduction of Georgiana Darcy. For neither had he any feeling. We might say that, like Collins, Wickham is a selfish character who only cares about outward appearances and has no good feelings. But, unlike Collins, he breaks the social code and is eventually exposed to the eyes of the world. *Social position:* Wickham's father was the steward of Darcy's father. He is not therefore of 'high birth', and his immoral habits make him squander the chances open to him: of rising in the Church or the Law. He even fails to marry the heiress he was pursuing.

Lydia Bennet

The youngest daughter, Lydia yet has the most to say. Almost her first words are: '. . . though I *am* the youngest, I'm the tallest'. As Elizabeth takes after her father, she is most like her mother. Her mother had liked soldiers once, and Lydia's favourite occupation is walking to Meryton to flirt with the officers.

'A stout, well-grown girl of fifteen, with a fine complexion and good humoured countenance . . . She had high animal spirits, and a sort of natural self-consequence.'

Later, Elizabeth thinks Lydia 'untamed'. She is like a domestic animal which has not been trained. Allowed by her mother to do as she pleases, and worst of all, encouraged in her unrestrained behaviour with men, she ends up living with a man with no thought of marrying him. She is too young to understand even the social morality accepted amongst her class. Elizabeth's judgement of her is probably Jane Austen's: she is 'ignorant, idle and vain'.

Charlotte Lucas

Charlotte is sensible and intelligent, and Elizabeth's best friend. But she is plain in appearance and realises her chances of marriage are not great. She is twenty-seven. She accepts Collins because she fears she will not be married otherwise. Her view of marriage is therefore completely unromantic. She thinks happiness in marriage is completely a matter of chance. She is too intelligent for Collins, and Elizabeth is probably right that she cannot be happy with him. But Charlotte does not demand the same kind of happiness as Elizabeth. Like so many of the other characters, Charlotte is rather materialistic.

Social position: having no fortune, Charlotte is in a difficult position, for she is plain as well. In Jane Austen's time, a woman who remained unmarried would almost inevitably be worse off than if she married. It explains why so many of the female characters are pre-occupied with the material advantages of marriage.

Caroline Bingley and Mrs Hurst

The Bingley sisters are rich and proud: 'They were in fact very fine ladies; not deficient in good humour when they were pleased, nor in the power of being agreeable where they chose it; but proud and conceited.'

Mrs Hurst does not otherwise play any significant part in the novel. Miss Bingley, however, supports Darcy in getting Bingley away from Jane, and is herself very jealous of Darcy and Elizabeth. Another materialistic character who criticises Elizabeth for her low manners and consistently points out the inferior social position of the Bennets and their relatives, Miss Bingley is badly behaved herself. She backbites when Elizabeth leaves the room, and is hypocritical in pretending to be Jane's friend. She tries flattery and allurement to win Darcy, but is no match for Elizabeth's intelligence. She is driven to desperate insults and impolite behaviour when Elizabeth and she meet at Pemberley.

Lady Catherine de Bourgh

Lady Catherine is an egotist. She is wholly conscious of her own self-importance and the need for her rank to be respected. She always gives her opinion and does not expect to be contradicted. She behaves in an insensitive way, ordering everyone's lives. She asks Elizabeth impolite, impertinent questions at Rosings.

She displays her worst behaviour when she tries to bully Elizabeth into a promise not to become engaged to her nephew, Darcy. Lady Catherine dismisses her as 'a young woman of inferior birth, of no importance in the world'.

Social position: part of the lesser aristocracy, Lady Catherine shows this class at its most materialistic and ill-bred. She wishes to unite Rosings and Pemberley by marrying her daughter to Darcy. This was quite a common thing amongst the aristocracy. Lady Catherine does not care about marriage for love.

The Lucases

Sir William Lucas has risen by trade. Having been knighted (and so presented once at Court) he has retired to enjoy his wealth. He is as materialistic as most of the others, but being a weak, simple character, he is not unlikeable.

Lady Lucas is no more intelligent than Mrs Bennet. She enjoys her short-lived triumph when Charlotte marries Mr Collins and she can thus speculate about her being mistress of Longbourn.

Kitty and Mary Bennet

Both daughters are badly brought up. Kitty is 'weak-spirited, irritable, completely under Lydia's guidance'. Mary studies hard because she is the only plain daughter, but 'had neither genius nor taste'. She plays the piano with vanity and affectation, and is the only one of the Bennets who thinks anything of Mr Collins's abilities. However, Kitty, we learn at the end of the novel, has the chance to improve by often visiting her married sisters.

The Gardiners

'Mr Gardiner was a sensible, gentlemanlike man, greatly superior to his sister as well by nature as education.'

Mrs Gardiner is 'an amiable, intelligent, elegant woman, and a great favourite with all her Longbourn nieces'.

The superior manners of Elizabeth's uncle and aunt are an asset to Elizabeth when they meet Darcy at Pemberley. Darcy sees she has some sensible relatives. The Gardiners guess that Darcy loves Elizabeth but are too polite to mention it. Mrs Gardiner praises Darcy's character in her letter to Elizabeth and sees they are well-suited.

Social position: Mr Gardiner is in trade and lives in Cheapside, an 'unfashionable' part of London. Although from the same background as Mrs Bennet and Aunt Philips, he has a refined, educated character. Also, from the amount he is able to do for Lydia, we see Mr Gardiner has money and practical sense.

Mrs Philips

Married to the former clerk of her attorney-father, Mrs Philips is more genial, but no more intelligent than Mrs Bennet. She is awed by Mr Collins.

Miss de Bourgh

The heiress of a large fortune, Lady Catherine's daughter is, however, 'pale and sickly', and carefully guarded by her companion, Mrs Jenkinson. She never says anything.

Colonel Fitzwilliam

The younget son of a Lord, Colonel Fitzwilliam is well-bred and likeable. But he must marry for money to keep up his social position, otherwise he would have been even more attracted to Elizabeth. As Darcy's cousin, he is joint-guardian over Miss Darcy.

Georgiana Darcy

Miss Darcy is called 'proud' by Wickham; he does this in just the same way that he blackens her brother's reputation. She narrowly escaped Wickham's evil designs on her by confessing to her brother. She is shy, and is only sixteen. In the end, we are told, Elizabeth and she grow to be great friends.

Mr Hurst

'He was an indolent man, who lived only to eat, drink, and play at cards.'

Discussion of aspects of the characters

'For herself she was humbled; but she was proud of him'; 'By you, I was properly humbled'. These two quotations describe the similar effects Darcy and Elizabeth had upon each other. How is it that each character 'humbled' the pride of the other?

Points that could be used in answering this question are:

(1) You might divide your answer into a comparison of how Darcy was humbled by Elizabeth; how Elizabeth was humbled by Darcy.

(2) Darcy is very proud, but also generous. When Elizabeth says 'had you behaved in a more gentleman-like manner', he realises that his pride had made him certain of her accepting his marriage proposal. His generous nature makes him realise that she is a better woman and he had insulted her by such a proposal.

(3) Elizabeth learns from Darcy's letter that she has based her opinion of him on a misfounded prejudice. All that Wickham told her had been wrong. Realising her error, Elizabeth is humbled.

(4) Elizabeth feels gratitude that Darcy should have asked her to marry him. She respects him after understanding his true behaviour toward Wickham. When she learns of what he has done for Lydia, she is truly humbled. She recognises his generosity even more.

(5) Both characters have reason to be 'proud' of the other. Elizabeth realises Darcy's true worth. Darcy realises that Elizabeth's qualities are worth humbling his pride for.

'One has got all good qualities, and the other all the appearance of it'. Show how just an assessment this is of the characters of Darcy and Wickham.

Points that could be used in answering this question are:

(1) You might divide your answer into a comparison of how Darcy has many good qualities which he does not show; how Wickham has the appearance of having good qualities, but behaves with none.

(2) Darcy has aloof and haughty manners. His behaviour makes him unpopular. Elizabeth thinks he is being critical of her because he appears severe. He appears to her to have the worst kind of pride in separating Jane and Bingley.

(3) Darcy has been brought up to have proud manners, but he is a good friend to those who know him. He is a good brother to his sister, and a good master to his servants. He helps the poor. He is shy by nature and is unable to speak about his deepest feelings. He behaves justly toward Wickham. He arranges Lydia's marriage.

(4) Wickham is very handsome, has excellent manners, is clever, and says everything well. He appears to be modest and not to want to expose Darcy. He appears to have been wronged by Darcy.

(5) Wickham tries to seduce Miss Darcy to spite Darcy because he had not given Wickham the living he wanted. He runs up many gambling debts. He wastes the money given to him to study the law. He seduces Lydia without intending to marry her. He blackens Darcy's character by telling untruths.

Structure and style

The plot

Most critics agree that Jane Austen had great skill in constructing her plots. What is a plot? At its simplest level, it is the plan of a novel, the way an author maps out the story he has to tell. If we consider how Jane Austen does this, in *Pride and Prejudice*, first of all we see that she is telling the love story of the two young people. This story falls into an easily observed symmetry:

(1) The first part deals with the meeting of Darcy and Elizabeth, and shows how they form impressions of each other, and how Darcy eventually becomes so much in love that he asks Elizabeth to marry him. The climax of the first part is Darcy's proposal at Hunsford and Elizabeth's rejection of it.

(2) The second part shows how both of the lovers come to a far better understanding of each other. Their acquaintance is renewed and they are about to become united when an obstacle appears which threatens to ruin their affection. However, this is overcome and they are united at last.

This is a bare outline of the main plot. There are also sub-plots which, in some way or another, influence the main plot. For example:

(1) Bingley's courtship of Jane. This runs parallel with Darcy's courtship of Elizabeth. The most important point at which they interreact is when Darcy's influence separates Bingley and Jane, and this in turn strengthens Elizabeth's prejudice against Darcy. But even earlier in the novel, Jane's stay at Netherfield (which is for Bingley's sake) brings Elizabeth into the view of Darcy.

(2) Charlotte Lucas's marriage with Collins. This is necessary because

it causes Elizabeth to go to Kent where she again meets Darcy. Collins's patroness, Lady Catherine de Bourgh, is Darcy's aunt. This is a further example of Jane Austen's careful creation of the novel's plot.

(3) Darcy's relations with Wickham. Much of this has already taken place before the novel begins. At Meryton, Wickham prejudices Elizabeth against Darcy. She learns from Darcy's letter the truth about Wickham, and this strengthens her regard for Darcy. But Wickham's elopement with Lydia delays Darcy's second proposal to Elizabeth.

The other characters all have their place in the plot, and contribute to the main story. Nothing happens which we might consider unnatural. Indeed, so skilful are Jane Austen's plot technique and her characterisation that they cannot be considered apart.

Characterisation

Although the characters in *Pride and Prejudice* are varied and interesting for their own sakes, in the way they relate to each other they add to our appreciation of the story. For example:

(1) Wickham appears to have all the good qualities, whereas Darcy really has them. Wickham is in fact the opposite, or antithesis, of Darcy. Both turn out the opposite to how they seemed.

(2) Miss Bingley looks like, and seems to have the manners of, a lady, whilst Elizabeth often does 'unladylike' things. But her continual criticism of Elizabeth, and her hypocritical behaviour toward Jane, show that hers is a false gentility. Elizabeth, in comparison, though lively and not always conventional, proves to be a fitter wife for the well-bred Darcy.

(3) Mr Collins's courtship of Elizabeth, and then Charlotte, adds comedy to the novel. But it makes us compare:

   (i) Elizabeth's attitude to marriage and Charlotte's. Elizabeth's refusal, in comparison with Charlotte's acceptance, shows us the greater sense of Elizabeth, as well as her high ideals.

   (ii) Mr Collins's pride and Darcy's pride. Although Collins's proposal to Elizabeth is highly ridiculous, it can be compared to Darcy's first proposal later on. Both are quite sure they will be accepted, and both make hardly any appeal to Elizabeth's feelings.

These are just a few examples of how vital it is to see the care and subtlety that went into Jane Austen's plots and characterisation.

Dialogue

A skilful author makes his characters reveal a lot about themselves through what they say. Mrs Bennet is the most talkative character in the novel, and almost every time she speaks we expect her to reveal her lack of sense and the emptiness of her mind. In this example of her conversation, we see Mrs Bennet's main pre-occupations and weaknesses:

'For my part, Mr Bingley, *I* always keep servants that can do their own work; *my* daughters are brought up differently. But every body is to judge for themselves, and the Lucases are very good sort of girls, I assure you. It is a pity they are not handsome! Not that *I* think Charlotte so *very* plain—but then she is our particular friend.'
'She seems a very pleasant young woman', said Bingley.
'Oh! dear, yes;—but you must own she is very plain. Lady Lucas herself has often said so, and envied me Jane's beauty . . .' (Volume 1 Chapter 9)

Mrs Bennet is praising her own daughters to Mr Bingley, and intends that he should compare them at the same time with the Lucas girls. At first she condescendingly says Charlotte Lucas is not very plain; but when Bingley pays Miss Lucas a compliment, Mrs Bennet immediately reverses what she has said, calls Charlotte 'very plain', and compares her not very subtlely to her beautiful Jane. Mrs Bennet's speeches always reflect her mind: they ramble on with no obvious direction except the general theme of her daughters' superiority.

Discussion of aspects of the dialogue

What do we learn of the two speakers from the following dialogue?:

'I remember hearing you once say, Mr Darcy, that you hardly ever forgave, that your resentment once created was unappeasable. You are very cautious, I suppose, as to its *being created*.'
'I am', said he, with a firm voice.
'And never allow yourself to be blinded by prejudice?'
'I hope not.'
'It is particularly incumbent on those who never change their opinion, to be secure of judging properly at first.'
'May I ask to what these questions tend?'
'Merely to the illustration of *your* character,' said she, endeavouring to shake off her gravity. 'I am trying to make it out.'
'And what is your success?'
She shook her head. 'I do not get on at all. I hear such different accounts of you as puzzle me exceedingly.'

'I can readily believe,' he answered gravely, 'that report may vary greatly with respect to me; and I could wish, Miss Bennet, that you were not to sketch my character at the present moment, as there is reason to fear that the performance would reflect no credit on either.'

'But if I do not take your likeness now, I may never have another opportunity.'

'I could by no means suspend any pleasure of yours,' he coldly replied. (Volume 1 Chapter 18)

Points that could be used in answering this question are:

(1) This discussion takes place during a dance at the Netherfield ball. Darcy and Elizabeth have become acquainted through Jane's illness and stay at Netherfield. Elizabeth has recently heard Wickham's story accusing Darcy, among other things, of pride.

(2) Elizabeth's questions are direct, and Darcy's answers are short and guarded.

(3) The author's descriptive touches are often important: Elizabeth endeavours 'to shake off her gravity'. This implies her questions are partly 'mock-serious'. Darcy, however, takes them very seriously. He answers 'gravely', with distant formality.

(4) Elizabeth shows her 'quickness' and 'wit' when she says: 'But if I do not take your likeness now, I may never have another opportunity.' Darcy's cold reply shows that he has been offended.

(5) Note that the whole dialogue centres around Darcy's proud character, and the proposition his 'resentment once created was unappeasable'. In fact, Elizabeth's remark is just as applicable to herself, for her resentment against Darcy, though not unappeasable, does prove an obstacle to the development of their relationship.

(6) When you are asked such a question on dialogue, you should always try to remember:

    (*i*) Where the passage occurs in the novel.

    (*ii*) What happens afterwards, so that you can relate it to later developments in the story as we have done in note (5). Remember that Jane Austen nearly always 'thinks ahead' in her dialogue.

So we can see how significant dialogue is in *Pride and Prejudice*. Some useful points to remember about dialogue are:

(1) Dialogue is used to reveal the character of its speakers.

(2) It can add drama to the story (note the dialogues between Darcy and Elizabeth especially; for example, Darcy's proposal of marriage).

(3) It often adds humour (for example, in the speeches of Mr Collins).

(4) Jane Austen's dialogue is usually 'realistic'; it is what the people in her world would have spoken, only it has been 'polished' (made more pure) by the author. (For example, Lydia's dialogue in Volume 2 Chapter 16)

Humour, irony and satire

Elizabeth is probably the mouthpiece of Jane Austen when she says: 'I hope I never ridicule what is wise or good. Follies and nonsense, whims and inconsistencies *do* divert me, I own, and I laugh at them whenever I can' (Volume 1 Chapter 11). Like Elizabeth, Jane Austen was fascinated by human character. Her intelligent sense of humour especially enabled her to see the 'follies and nonsense, whims and inconsistencies' of the people she portrayed. Her treatment of Mrs Bennet, Mr Collins and Lydia are fine examples. We can say that she laughs at the follies and nonsense of these characters without being cruel or unfair.

However, her use of irony and satire is more serious. In the passage that follows, Wickham and Elizabeth are talking about Darcy and his sister. Wickham has just married Lydia, and Elizabeth now understands him very well.

'. . . Did you see him while you were at Lambton? I thought I understood from the Gardiners that you had.'
'Yes; he introduced us to his sister.'
'And do you like her?'
'Very much.'
'I have heard, indeed, that she is uncommonly improved within this year or two. When I last saw her, she was not very promising. I am very glad you liked her. I hope she will turn out well.'
'I dare say she will; she has got over the most trying age.' (Volume 3 Chapter 10)

This is a fine example of Jane Austen's irony. It expresses its meaning indirectly, through what only *appears* to be polite conversation. We see that:

(1) Wickham is unsure how much Elizabeth now knows about Darcy and himself.
(2) Wickham says when he last saw Miss Darcy she was 'unpromising'. Yet both he and Elizabeth know that at that time he tried to seduce her.
(3) Wickham says he hopes Miss Darcy 'will turn out well'. Elizabeth's reply caps the irony. Miss Darcy has 'got over the most trying age', that is, the innocent age when she is in danger of being deceived by men like Wickham.

Satire makes use of humour and irony, and, in Jane Austen, usually has a social meaning. For instance, we learn about Bingley's sisters: 'They were of a respectable family in the north of England; a circumstance more deeply impressed in their memories than that their brother's fortune and their own had been acquired by trade.' (Volume 1 Chapter 4).

The irony here is that we remember how Miss Bingley criticises Elizabeth and Jane because they have an uncle who lives near Cheapside —a business area of London. Yet her brother's fortune has been 'acquired by trade'. Jane Austen is satirising the snobbishness of attitudes like Miss Bingley's.

The author is detached and unsentimentally ironic. Mrs Bennet, Lydia, Mr Collins, and Lady Catherine, are not spared for their failings. Like Elizabeth, she laughs at her characters' follies, but her judgement is always sure and never, like Mr Bennet's, irresponsible.

Further points for study

(1) Look at Mr Bennet's use of humour and irony. Does the author *always* agree with him?
(2) How does Jane Austen satirise Lady Catherine de Bourgh? What is she saying about the kind of behaviour Lady Catherine stands for?
(3) Why is Collins a ridiculous character?

In all these questions, you should find some examples and try to explain what the author is doing by using similar methods to the above.

Themes

Love and marriage

The main theme of *Pride and Prejudice*, as in all of Jane Austen's novels, is the choice people make for marriage partners. Especially, it is about the difficulties two people have to overcome before they marry. Elizabeth and Darcy have to understand and overcome their own 'pride and prejudice' before they become suitable marriage partners. Elizabeth is attractive, individual and intelligent; Darcy is rich and handsome. But both have to gain self-knowledge, for Darcy is proud and will not demean himself, and Elizabeth is too hasty in her judgement and liable to be taken in by appearances—such as Darcy's haughty exterior, and Wickham's easy manner. Although Elizabeth does not set out to captivate Darcy, her lively mind, affectionate nature, and pretty eyes soon have this effect. Even though his pride is greatly offended by her low social standing, and her family's behaviour, Darcy proposes marriage. But he has yet to humble himself, for he believes that Elizabeth will accept him because he is so superior. She misunderstand's Darcy's behaviour and character owing to her prejudice in favour of Wickham. Darcy is only seen through Elizabeth's eyes and those of society—only at the end do we learn what his feelings were at crucial points in the story. The events which occur in the novel eventually help them to realise their mistakes, and to esteem each other's character. Thus, their marriage is founded on affection and understanding, and is not the result of an immediate, blind impulse.

We can measure this main love story against the standards of the other marriages in *Pride and Prejudice*.

Charlotte Lucas and Collins. Being twenty-seven and plain-looking, Charlotte does not have a high view of marriage. She tells Elizabeth: 'Happiness in marriage is entirely a matter of chance.' She has few hopes of happiness in marriage beyond the material comfort it can give, and so she marries a man who is inferior in intelligence, only for the home and position he offers. Collins only wants a wife because in the eyes of society it is time for him to settle and be married. Lady Catherine has advised him to marry, and he quickly changes his affections from Jane to Elizabeth, and from Elizabeth to Charlotte. His feelings are totally imaginary. Elizabeth is most disappointed because she knows Charlotte could not be happy with such a husband.

Mr and Mrs Bennet. Mr Bennet 'captivated by youth and beauty, and that appearance of good humour, which youth and beauty generally give, had married a woman whose weak understanding and illiberal mind, had very early in their marriage put an end to all real affection for her.' (Volume 2 Chapter 19) More than this, she had no money. So from every point of view their marriage is a failure. Its consequences are seen in the bad marriage Lydia makes, for Lydia is like her mother.

Lydia and Wickham. Wickham tried to seduce Miss Darcy, and marry Miss King—both heiresses. He elopes with Lydia with no intention of marrying her and is only made to do this by Darcy's intervention. Lydia is too ignorant to understand the damage her elopment would do to her reputation if she did not marry Wickham. They are 'a couple who were only brought together because their passions were stronger than their virtue'. We learn at the end that Wickham's 'affection for her soon sunk into indifference; her's lasted a little longer'.

Jane and Bingley. The marriage of Jane and Bingley is based on good foundations. They are attracted at once, and have the fortune to have similar, easy dispositions. Bingley also has a lot of money.

Discussion of the theme of marriage

Who do you think make the most successful marriages in *Pride and Prejudice*? Points that could be used in answering this question are:

(1) List the necessary qualities for a good marriage according to the novel:

  (*i*) understanding each other's character

  (*ii*) good disposition of the partners

  (*iii*) similarity in feeling and taste
  (*iv*) affection, attraction
  (*v*) a lot of money

(2) Mention the bad points in the unsuccessful marriages. for example, Lydia's and Wickham's irresponsibility; Mrs Bennet's bad temper and ignorance compared to Mr Bennet's superior intelligence; Charlotte's intelligence and Collins's stupidity.
(3) Show how Jane and Bingley, and Elizabeth and Darcy have the qualities described in (1).

Good breeding and social rank

The question whether nobility and gentility are confined only to persons of high rank is an old theme in English literature. It figures in all of Jane Austen's novels, for although she did not reject the hierarchical standards of social rank current in her time, she was an intelligent observer of human society. This made her ask whether what went in the clothes of fashionable gentility really was genteel. Part 1 of these Notes suggested that Jane Austen accepted the social standards of her age. This means she did not wish to change society so that, say, all men were considered equal. She accepted the world of Lords and Ladies, aristocracy and gentry, clergyman and landowners; and rarely introduces servants or working people. However, while she thought wealth desirable, she did not believe that wealthy people were necessarily always the most cultured; and while she would have defended the Church, she was not blind to the worldliness of a clergyman like Collins.

  What did Jane Austen understand by 'gentility', and, who, in her eyes, was 'a lady'? The following discussion between Darcy, Elizabeth and Miss Bingley is helpful:

'. . . A woman [says Miss Bingley] must have a thorough knowledge of music, singing, drawing, dancing, and the modern languages, to deserve the word; and besides all this, she must possess a certain something in her air and manner of walking, the tone of her voice, her address and expressions, or the word will be but half deserved.'
'All this she must possess,' added Darcy, 'and to all this she must yet add something more substancial, in the improving of her mind by extensive reading.'
'I am no longer surprised at your knowing *only* six accomplished women. I rather wonder now at your knowing *any*.' [says Elizabeth].
                (Volume 1 Chapter 8)

Darcy and Miss Bingley list all the qualities they think a lady should have. Elizabeth thinks that hardly any women can have all these. Miss

Bingley herself is a fashionable lady with well-bred manners. However, we see she is not above snobbishly criticising Jane and Elizabeth when they are not in the room; and later, when she realises Darcy is in love with Elizabeth, she makes unkind personal remarks about her, and is so ill-mannered as to remain silent when Elizabeth and Mrs Gardiner call on Miss de Bourgh at Pemberley.

In comparison, Elizabeth is intelligent, but unconventional. Her walk to Netherfield to see Jane when she is unwell is not 'ladylike'. We see from the above passage that she disagrees with Darcy and Miss Bingley about what a lady should be like. *Pride and Prejudice* has been praised especially for the character of Elizabeth. We learn that she is attractive and individual enough to make Darcy love her despite his social pride. Although Elizabeth is not 'perfect', Jane Austen clearly likes her the best, and we can conclude that Elizabeth, with her mixture of intelligence, affectionateness, and playful unconventionality, is the author's own idea of a very likeable person who is also 'a lady'.

What are the qualities which Jane Austen valued? Elizabeth has affection for Jane and her father, has common sense, good taste, and is not overawed by wealth. She sees her mother's and her younger sisters' bad-breeding, and her advice to Mr Bennet not to let Lydia go to Brighton is very sensible. She reads books and appreciates lovely scenery. In short, she is as accomplished, and 'genteel', as any girl from a richer family.

In the other characters, we see a different valuation of 'gentility' and 'nobility'. To begin with, Darcy is so proud of his own social standing that he refuses to mix with those lower than himself. Even when he falls in love with Elizabeth, he cannot forget she is lower in society than himself. Miss Bingley praises Darcy by expressing the social judgements she thinks he would make. However, under the influence of Elizabeth his pride is softened and by the end of the novel we learn that she is even able 'to take liberties' with him. Lady Catherine de Bourgh is even prouder than Darcy. But despite all her wealth and the loftiness of her social rank, she is ill-bred, for she treats everyone else with self-importance and unconcern for their feelings. Her wealth and rank make her 'gentility' mere outward show, and there is no true nobility in her manners. Characters like Sir William Lucas, Mr Collins, and Mrs Bennet, are simply dazzled by the show of wealth and do not know true nobility or gentility. Charlotte Lucas, though intelligent, also puts too high a value on material possessions and does not believe in noble motives. In contrast, Charles Bingley does not care about Jane's relatives in Cheapside, and even tolerates Mrs Bennet. Jane, also, thinks well of everyone and displays no social snobbery.

Further points for study

(1) '*Pride and Prejudice* is about what people are really like, and what they think they are like.' Discuss the characters of (*i*) Miss Bingley (*ii*) Sir William Lucas and (*iii*) Lady Catherine de Bourgh in this light.

(2) Give an account of the visit of Lady Catherine to Longbourn and her interview with Elizabeth. What does this tell us about their respective, good breeding?

(3) Give some examples of Elizabeth's unconventional behaviour. Do they make her 'ungenteel'?

Moral standards

The moral standards of Jane Austen's time were strict, but not always strongly enforced. Thus, Lydia *has* to be married to Wickham, despite his bad character, because otherwise she would never be accepted again in society. Elizabeth and Jane also realise that, in such a case, their own reputations would be harmed by their sister's behaviour. Lady Catherine and Mr Collins both interpret society's moral code in a prudish, vindictive manner in the way that they condemn Lydia, and wish her behaviour to hurt her sisters' reputations.

Jane Austen accepted society's moral code which, we should remember, came originally from the teachings of Christianity. She comments that Collins's remark that Lydia should be forgiven, but never be spoken to again, is 'unchristian'.

So we can see that the moral code is understood in a different spirit by Jane Austen. She also shared the moral viewpoints described in Part 1 of these Notes, as 'classical'. That is, she believed the passions should be controlled by reason. Therefore, the moral outlook of her novels can be summed up like this:

(1) Feelings are meant to be governed by reason and by following the moral laws accepted by society and taught by religion. Those characters who follow their passions, or have no powers of reason, are criticised (for example, Wickham and Lydia).

(2) The standards of society are not to be broken, but while some characters (such as Collins, Lady Catherine, and Miss Bingley) follow them blindly to flatter their own social standing and show how good they are, the intelligent ones (such as Elizabeth and the Gardiners) use them as the measure of good sense and propriety.

Discussion of moral themes

(1) Discuss the moral vision of *Pride and Prejudice*. NOTE: You should try to understand the above, then find examples from the characters in the book showing different moral views. You should weigh these against what you think Jane Austen is saying.

(2) 'Good sense and comfortable living'—does Jane Austen believe in anything more?

Points to think about in answering these questions:

(*i*) This type of question is really asking what *you* think about the novel. Jane Austen has been criticised for being nearly as materialistic as her characters, and this question is asking you if you agree.

(*ii*) You might divide your answer into a discussion of the unintelligent, materialistic characters; and the intelligent characters. Are the intelligent characters as concerned about rank and wealth as the others? If so, and you think the author agrees with them, then your answer to Question 2 will be no. If you think her characters believe in something more, what do you think it is?

Summary on themes

We have seen that 'themes' are what the book is about, or 'what it is saying'. Thus they can tell us a lot about an author as well as his characters. The main themes of the novel are:

(*i*) Love and marriage
(*ii*) Good breeding and social rank
(*iii*) Moral belief and behaviour.

Part 4

Hints for study

General remarks

When answering examination questions remember that, first, your knowledge of the book, and second, your understanding of it are being tested. It is essential to know the book well. You must:

(1) Know the story in outline, and be able to fit an extract into its context in the book.
(2) Be able to show a knowledge of details when discussing the behaviour, character and opinions of the characters, as well as in dealing with the literary technique.
(3) Be able to support your points or argument with suitable quotations.

Points for close study

Themes

The themes of a novel are what its subject is; what it is about. We have seen in Part 3 what the main themes are in *Pride and Prejudice*. Try to find some extracts which further illustrate the themes. Here are some examples:

Marriage

Volume 1 Chapter 6. Charlotte and Elizabeth are discussing marriage. Charlotte has noticed that Bingley and Jane are obviously attracted, and suggests Jane should encourage him. Elizabeth says this is not in Jane's nature, and she should not attract a man before knowing first if he will make a suitable husband. Charlotte thinks happiness in marriage is only a question of luck anyway, and so to try to know one's partner before marriage is no help, because characters change so much after marriage.

SIGNIFICANT POINTS:
(1) The discussion tells us a lot about the attitude to marriage of Elizabeth, Charlotte, and Jane.
(2) Elizabeth believes marriage should be founded upon mutual understanding, and not entered into merely for the sake of wealth.

(3) Charlotte's attitude to marriage is the opposite. She takes a low view of the chances of happiness, and thinks it better to get the richest husband one can.

(4) See from this particular part of the novel how each character does eventually find the marriage partner he or she is looking for.

Breeding

Volume 1 Chapter 17. The whole chapter should be studied. Concentrate on the behaviour of the Bennet family, Mr Collins, Miss Bingley and Mr Darcy. It would be useful if you described the behaviour of each of these characters in a few words and remembered it.

QUESTION:

Give an account of the Netherfield ball, emphasising particularly the 'good' or 'bad' breeding of the most important characters.

Points you could use in your answer:

(1) Mention the bad breeding of the Bennet family; in Mary's singing, Mr Bennet's interruption, and Mrs Bennet's talk.

(2) Comment on the proud, formal bearing of Darcy, and the snobbery of Miss Bingley's remarks, and of the Bingley sisters at the end of the evening.

(3) Discuss the long, absurdly formal self-introduction of Collins to Darcy, and the effect it has.

(4) Describe the role of the whole chapter for the development of the novel, and the part its theme of breeding plays.

Setting

The setting of *Pride and Prejudice* is the social life of the kind of people whom Jane Austen knew best. Their environment is rural, and their social life is a mixture of parties, balls and visits. You should describe for your own benefit the kind of thing which happens at each of these, and consider the context in which they occur in the book.

(1) A party—a small gathering where the people present entertain themselves by playing cards, dancing, or playing the piano, normally after the evening meal.

(2) A ball—a larger gathering mainly for dancing.

(3) Visits—short visits for a few hours (like those of Darcy and Bingley to Longbourn), or long stays for weeks or months (like Elizabeth's visit to Hunsford).

QUESTIONS ON SETTING:

(1) What kind of social life do the characters lead in *Pride and Prejudice*?

(2) Describe any *two* houses in *Pride and Prejudice*.

NOTE: look up references to Longbourn, Hunsford, Pemberley, and Rosings, and make notes on the life their inhabitants lead, and their social rank. (Remember that Mr Collins is a clergyman, Mr Bennet a country-gentleman, and Darcy has a large fortune and a house in town, as well as owning Pemberley.)

Character

We have already seen how much observation Jane Austen put into her characters. Study Volume 2 Chapter 16 and make notes on Lydia's character, then look at her letter in Volume 3 Chapter 5. Then answer the following question by discussing Lydia.

QUESTION:
'The behaviour of Jane Austen's characters is what we are prepared to expect'—discuss.

Conflict

Make notes on the conflicts between the following characters:

(i)   Elizabeth and Miss Bingley
(ii) Darcy and Wickham
(iii) Lady Catherine and Elizabeth

Observe how these conflicts add to the drama of the novel, and how they add to the development of the plot.

For example: the effect Miss Bingley's conflict with Elizabeth has on Darcy's love for Elizabeth is to display Elizabeth's greater intelligence and her more lively character. At Pemberley, Miss Bingley's bad behaviour only shows Darcy how superior Elizabeth is.

Climax

The climaxes in *Pride and Prejudice* are easy to find if you remember the turning points of the story—for instance, Darcy's proposal of marriage; Lydia's elopement with Wickham. A climax is always the result of something that has gone before. Jane Austen prepares her readers for Darcy's proposal by his frequent visits to the Parsonage, and his 'accidental' meetings with Elizabeth when she is out walking. You can find similar examples for yourself for Lydia's elopement with Wickham.

QUESTION:
What part do the climaxes play in *Pride and Prejudice*?

Selection and use of quotations

For a novel it is pointless to learn long quotations because you will probably forget them. It is better to know quite a lot of short ones which you will easily remember. Jane Austen is a very suitable novelist for this, as she often uses short sentences which are full of meaning and often sum up a whole chapter or character.

Character

See how often, at the first mention of a character, Jane Austen will use one or more telling sentences in description. For example:

BINGLEY: 'Mr Bingley was good looking and gentlemanlike; he had a pleasant countenance, and easy, unaffected manners.' (Volume 1 Chapter 3)

MR BENNET: 'Mr Bennet was so odd a mixture of quick parts, sarcastic humour, reserve, and caprice, that the experience of three and twenty years had been insufficient to make his wife understand his character.' (Volume 1 Chapter 2) (You do not need to use the whole sentence; for example, Mr Bennet was an 'odd mixture of quick parts, sarcastic humour, reserve and caprice . . .' When you reduce a quotation, however, you must make quite sure that it is still accurate, that is makes sense in the sentence where you wish to use it, and that you have not in any way altered the meaning of the full original quotation.)

ELIZABETH: '. . . she had a lively, playful disposition, which delighteu in any thing ridiculous.' (Volume 1 Chapter 3).

DARCY AND BINGLEY: '. . . In understanding Darcy was the superior. Bingley was by no means deficient, but Darcy was clever. He was at the same time haughty, reserved, and fastidious, and his manners, though well bred, were not inviting . . . *Bingley was sure of being liked wherever he appeared, Darcy was continually giving offence.*' (Volume 1 Chapter 4) The last sentence is a fine example of one which gives a lot of vital information for the book, and is quite short. The one before it could be broken up so: Darcy 'was . . . haughty, reserved, and fastidious, and his manners, though well bred, were not inviting.'

There are many other telling quotations which you could use to show Jane Austen's insight into characters, or which can sum up a character in their own words. Thus, Collins as a lover is summed up by his own unconsciously ironic statement: 'I can assure the young ladies that I come prepared to admire them.' (Volume 1 Chapter 14)

Turning-points and climaxes

When you have decided where the turning-points, climaxes, conflicts and so on, occur in the novel, go to the particular chapter or paragraph which you have found, and choose suitable sentences or phrases to quote. Notice, for instance, the following extracts from Volume 2 Chapter 13, where Elizabeth, having read Darcy's letter, proceeds to think about what it said. It is a turning-point for her estimation of Darcy:

> ... Her feelings as she read were scarcely to be defined. With amazement did she first understand that he believed any apology to be in his power; and stedfastly was she persuaded that he could have no explanation to give, which a just sense of shame would not conceal. *With a strong prejudice against every thing he might say*, she began his account of what had happened at Netherfield.

Notice how the sentence in italic sums up Elizabeth's first feelings when she read the letter. Then she re-reads it, and begins to have doubts about her acceptance of Wickham's story against Darcy. Finally, she has to admit that Darcy's account is the true one, and Wickham's picture of Darcy totally false:

> She grew absolutely ashamed of herself.—Of neither Darcy nor Wickham could she think, without feeling *she had been blind, partial, prejudiced, absurd.*

Again, the words in italic sum up Elizabeth's feelings at this point. Now, if you wished to sum up yourself this turning-point in the novel, you might write: 'When Elizabeth first reads Darcy's letter she is very much against him. She starts "with a strong prejudice against every thing he might say". But when she thinks about it more clearly, she realises that Darcy's story about Wickham is more likely to be true, and that Wickham's story was false. She knows she has misjudged them both, that she had been "blind, partial, prejudiced, absurd".'

Moral

The 'moral' of a story is where its message is to be found, or something very significant is being said. Quotations to show the moral of *Pride and Prejudice* will depend on your ability to recognise what the moral is, of course. We have already discussed Jane Austen's attitudes. Very often, however, she gives her message through another character, and Elizabeth is usually the one. For example, when in Volume 3 Chapter 13 she learns about the engagement of Jane and Bingley, Elizabeth's thoughts are these:

. . . and in spite of his [Bingley's] being a lover, Elizabeth really believed all his expectations of felicity to be *rationally founded*, because they had for basis the *excellent understanding*, and super-excellent disposition of Jane, and a *general similarity of feeling and taste* between her and himself.

The phrases italicised here can be put together in our own words, and the moral for the foundation of a good marriage can be established.

We can say: Jane Austen believed that for happiness to exist in marriage, it had to be 'rationally founded', based on an 'excellent understanding' between the couple, and 'a general similarity of feeling and taste' between them. All you need to remember are: 'rationally founded', 'excellent understanding', and 'a general similarity of feeling and taste'.

Sometimes, a character will sum up a very important part of the book. When Elizabeth and Jane are discussing Darcy and Wickham, having now understood the true facts about each, Elizabeth says: 'One has got all the goodness, and the other all the appearance of it'. Her quotation sums up the moral of the Darcy-Wickham part of the novel.

Points to remember about quotations:
(1) Keep them short; if necessary split up a sentence and just remember a few words or a phrase.
(2) Choose quotations which say something significant about a character, a situation, or show Jane Austen's successful literary technique.
(3) Use them to support a fact, or sum up your argument.

How to answer questions effectively

Remember the secret to answering any literary question successfully is first to understand what exactly you are being asked, and then to give your answer in the form of *an argument*.

An 'argument' is where you are able to show (*a*) that you understand the question (*b*) that you can bring forward enough evidence from the book to explain your answer. In a very simple question where, for example, you are asked to compare two characters, or say whether you think a character is good or bad, you can easily split your answer in two. In the first part of your answer you will put one side of the case, and in the second part the opposite side. You will then write a conclusion saying which character you think is better, or whether a character's 'good part' outweighs his 'bad part'. In both parts of your answer, you should bring forward quotations to support or sum up your points. Always argue from facts (that is, details and evidence from the book).

If the question is about a specific literary term, or terms, such as 'theme', 'irony', or 'plot', think of examples where the theme appears, or where irony is used, or the plot can be seen. Select your examples, then put them down in separate paragraphs, and finally sum up what you have written.

If you are asked to give a summary of the role of one character or one aspect of the story, start with a general paragraph stating what the main points are. Then take each point individually, and say more about it, including examples and quotations. You should try to avoid giving narrative answers alone, but rather show your understanding of a question by organising your answer in an argument.

Points to remember:
(1) Read the question carefully.
(2) Decide what your argument will be (you may wish to start by making a plan).
(3) Arrange your points in paragraphs bringing detailed evidence and quotations to your aid.
(4) End your argument by summing up what you have said, and making some concluding remarks.

Specimen questions and answers

The following questions are types that will probably occur in an examination on *Pride and Prejudice*. The answers given have had to be made shorter than your answers would be. See how they are constructed, how they answer the question asked, and try, if you can, to add more examples to the different arguments. The words added in brackets should help you to see how the material is organised.

---

(1) Write character studies of TWO minor characters in *Pride and Prejudice*, and show how they contribute to the novel.

[*General character description*] **Mr Gardiner** is the uncle of the Bennet girls, and the brother of Mrs Bennet. He is not like his sister, however, rather he is: 'a sensible, gentleman-like man, greatly superior to his sister as well by nature as education'.

He is a business man, and although he lives in an unfashionable part of London, he has both culture and good-breeding. He impresses Mr Darcy with his intelligent remarks and behaviour when they meet at Pemberley. Mr Darcy is surprised he is Elizabeth's uncle because all her other relatives are so badly behaved.

[*Examples of his character*] When Lydia elopes with Wickham, it is Mr Gardiner who is the most useful relative, and at first Mr Bennet and Elizabeth believe he has paid Wickham a lot of money to marry Lydia. Although he would have done this, it was, in fact, Darcy. However, Mr

Gardiner and Darcy were able to work together to achieve the best result, while Mr Bennet was helpless.

[*His function in the novel*] The primary role of Mr Gardiner in the novel is to show Darcy that Elizabeth has some sensible relatives. Both he and Mrs Gardiner are also very good companions for Elizabeth on her tour of Derbyshire, and fit very well into the social relations that Elizabeth has with the Darcys there. Mr Gardiner, for example, spends one morning fishing with the gentleman at Pemberley. He and his wife realise that Darcy loves Elizabeth, but are too well-bred to say anything before she does.

When Lydia elopes, the whole Bennet family falls into disarray, but Mr Gardiner is able to bring about a practical solution together with Darcy. Mr Gardiner's letter also aids the plot by telling Mr Bennet and Elizabeth about the marriage settlement. Finally, at the end of the novel, we learn that the Gardiners often visit Pemberley, thus emphasising the affection Elizabeth has for her well-bred uncle and aunt.

[*General character*] **Colonel Fitzwilliam** is nearly thirty, is not handsome but has excellent manners. He is the younger son of a Lord, and is also Darcy's cousin. He is joint-guardian with Darcy of Darcy's sister, Georgiana. Being the younger son of a Lord, he will not inherit the family estate, and therefore admits to Elizabeth that he must marry where there is money.

[*Contribution*] Fitzwilliam contributes to the plot of the novel by his relationship with Darcy. He knows the real character of Wickham, being joint-guardian of Miss Darcy, and can therefore prove Darcy's story against Wickham's. He also knows that Darcy has saved a friend making 'a most imprudent marriage', and tells Elizabeth during one of their conversations. He does not know for sure that it is Bingley, but it makes Elizabeth certain that Darcy has separated Bingley and Jane, and so prejudices her further against Darcy.

Fitzwilliam is a cultivated gentleman, and in showing his admiration of Elizabeth, makes us see even more how attractive a person she must be. They speak about travelling, books and music, and Fitzwilliam calls often at the parsonage on Elizabeth's account. Had she any fortune, he probably would have proposed marriage.

[*Conclusion–referring to both characters*] Both Mr Gardiner and Colonel Fitzwilliam are gentlemen, though one is a business man and the other an aristocrat. They show us how well-bred characters behave, and also play their parts in the plot. They are characters of whom Jane Austen approves, and she does not satirise or laugh at them.

Now answer the same question, this time writing about Kitty Bennet and Mrs Philips.

(2) 'Jane Austen portrays truthfully and intelligently the limited world which she knew best'—discuss.

[*Introduction—setting*] Jane Austen's world is confined to a small section of society comprising country gentry and lesser aristocracy in England, at the opening of the nineteenth century. They live in comfort in pleasant houses in the country, and their lives consist of visiting each other, amusing themselves, and holding balls. Jane Austen knew this kind of life very well because she was born into a clergyman's family in southern England, and attended balls herself. She also studied the people in this world with careful observation, often satirising their behaviour and attitudes. Although this was a narrow world, her novels bear out Elizabeth's words: '. . . people themselves alter so much, that there is something new to be observed in them for ever'.

[*Characters*] Her characters range from the proud, aristocratic Darcy, to the talkative, dull-witted Mrs Philips; from the good-natured Jane Bennet, to the jealous, hypocritical Miss Bingley.

[*Themes*] They speak about each other's property, their daughters' chances of marriage, and their own rank, good-breeding, and self-importance. The women are always looking for eligible husbands: 'It is a truth universally acknowledged, that a single man in possession of a good fortune, must be in want of a wife.' They love to attract the men at balls: 'To be fond of dancing was a certain step towards falling in love . . .' Jane Austen portrays the emotions of her feminine character as they fall in love.

[*Plot*] The story of *Pride and Prejudice* is about two young people who eventually marry. The plot develops the obstacles they have to overcome, including their own pride and prejudice. Their story is true to life, with no strange or sensational events in it. They are both natural people with personal failings, but who are intelligent enough, in the end, to understand each other and their own selves better.

[*Style*] *Pride and Prejudice* is told in clear and elegant prose. The description of the pattern of life among the characters is full of everyday details.

[*Dialogue*] There is much dialogue that tells us about the characters through their own mouths; it is real, naturalistic dialogue. For example, the ignorant Mrs Bennet expresses herself in long, meandering speeches, which say little except to reflect her empty-mindedness; while Darcy's speech is formal and reserved.

Note that this part of the essay has discussed the 'truthful portrayal' of Jane Austen's limited world. The next part will deal with her 'intelligent portrayal' of it.

Jane Austen's portrayal of her small world is therefore true to life. Her treatment of character is also intelligent. For example, Lady Catherine de Bourgh, who is proud of her aristocratic rank, and likes to show how important she is, really appears as a selfish, egotistical person. She asks Elizabeth a lot of impertinent questions, and shows her bad-breeding and egotism by interrupting Elizabeth and Colonel Fitzwilliam's private discussion. When she learns they are talking of music, she boasts: 'There are few people in England, I suppose, who have more true enjoyment of music than myself, or a better natural taste.'

[*Humour*] Jane Austen's observation of character is often humorous or ironic. Mr Collins is a ridiculous figure, who behaves with absurd formality and exaggerated ceremony.

[*Irony*] But he is also selfish and vain, and is often the source of Mr Bennet's sarcasm and irony. For example, when Collins's patroness, Lady Catherine, is at last defeated, and Darcy is to marry Elizabeth, Mr Bennet writes to Collins suggesting that he 'stand by the nephew. He has more to give.'

[*Wit*] Both Mr Bennet and Elizabeth Bennet are the characters through whom Jane Austen shows much of her wit and intelligence. Elizabeth holds long, witty conversations with the serious Darcy. She also reminds us of the author herself when she says: 'I hope I never ridicule what is wise or good. Follies and nonsense, whims and inconsistencies *do* divert me, I own, and I laugh at them whenever I can.'

[*Conclusion*] Therefore, although Jane Austen's world was limited to the small part of humanity she knew best, she portrays them with truthfulness, and makes us see what such people are really like. For she is an intelligent author, who sees beneath appearances, and criticises as well as laughs at the follies of human beings.

---

(3) Illustrate with examples the satire of *Pride and Prejudice.*

[*General remarks on use of satire*] Jane Austen uses satire to show up the vanity and conceit of her characters. Usually, it expresses their social snobbery, or wish to show their own superiority to others. Wealth and rank, so-called virtue and good-breeding, are the objects of her satire.

[*Particular examples*] Lady Catherine de Bourgh is satirised for her display of wealth and rank. She is shown to be really proud and ill-mannered. Although she boasts of her influence and her daughter's accomplishment, Miss de Bourgh is a protected, sickly girl. The servile Mr Collins is satirised for his flattery of Lady Catherine's wealth and rank, and his materialistic assessment of the price of the furniture in the houses he enters, and the superiority of grandeur and numbers.

The snobbish Bingley sisters are shown to be not so high as they wish to think. Although they come from a respectable family, their fortune comes from trade, like Mr Gardiner's, although they look down on Elizabeth and Jane's uncle.

Characters who like to think highly of themselves are made to look hypocritical. In the case of Sir William Lucas, they are made to look stupid. Having risen by trade as well, Sir William moves from the town of Meryton a little way outside, and always speaks about his 'presentation at Court'—the time he went to St James to be knighted by the King. Yet when he goes to Rosings, Jane Austen gently satirises his awed behaviour. He and his daughter are so impressed by Lady Catherine's rank and wealth they are afraid to speak.

[*Public opinion*] Even the attitudes of the Meryton people in general are satirised. At first, Wickham is 'universally liked', and everyone believes his story about Darcy because he is so agreeable, and Darcy's manners are so proud. But when Wickham's gambling debts are revealed, and his elopement known, 'everybody declared that he was the wickedest young man in the world, and everybody began to find out, that they had always distrusted the appearance of his goodness'.

[*Conclusion*] Therefore, we can see that Jane Austen satirises people's hypocrisy, vanity and stupidity. She shows up the difference between what they think they are, and what they are really like.

Part 5

Suggestions for further reading

The text

The text of *Pride and Prejudice* is available in several series, of which the Penguin Classics edition by Ronald Blythe, Penguin Books, Harmondsworth, 1978 (and later printings) and the Everyman Library edition, Dent, London, 1963 (and later printings) are easily available. These Notes are based on R. W. Chapman's edition, Oxford University Press, Oxford, 1970.

Other novels by Jane Austen

The Novels of Jane Austen. The Text based on Collation of the Early Editions, edited by R. W. Chapman, Clarendon Press, Oxford, six volumes, 1923–54. The definitive edition. Chapman's version of the text is also used in the World's Classics edition, Oxford University Press, Oxford, six volumes, 1907–31, 3rd edition, 1988.

Jane Austen's novels are also available in the following series: Collins Pocket Classics, Everyman's Library, Octopus and the Penguin English Library.

Bibliography

CHAPMAN, R. W.: *Jane Austen: A Critical Bibliography*, Oxford University Press, 1955.

Criticism

BUSH, DOUGLAS: *Jane Austen*, Macmillan, London, 1975.
BUTLER, MARILYN: *Jane Austen and the War of Ideas*, Clarendon Press, Oxford, 1975; paperback 1987.
CECIL, DAVID: *A Portrait of Jane Austen*, Constable, London, 1978; paperback by Penguin Books, Harmondsworth, 1980.
FERGUS, JAN: *Jane Austen and the Didactic Novel*, Macmillan, London, 1983.

GARD, ROGER: *Jane Austen's Novels: The Art of Clarity*, Yale University Press, New Haven, 1992.

GILLIE, OLIVER: *A Preface to Jane Austen*, revised edition, (Preface Books) Longman, Harlow, 1985.

GOONERATNE, YASMINE: *Jane Austen*, Cambridge University Press, Cambridge, 1970.

HALPERIN, JOHN: *The Life of Jane Austen*, Harvester, Brighton, 1984.

HARDY, BARBARA: *A Reading of Jane Austen*, Athlone Press, London, 1979.

KAPLAN, DEBORAH: *Jane Austen among Women*, Johns Hopkins University Press, Baltimore, 1993.

LASCELLES, MARY: *Jane Austen and Her Art*, Clarendon Press, Oxford, 1939.

MACDONAGH, OLIVER: *Jane Austen: Real and Imagined Worlds*, Yale University Press, New Haven and London, 1993.

MORGAN, SUSAN: *In the Meantime: Character and Perception in Jane Austen's Novels*, University of Chicago Press, Chicago, 1980.

MORRIS, IVOR: *Mr Collins Considered: Approaches to Jane Austen*, Routledge, London, 1987.

ODMARK, JOHN: *An Understanding of Jane Austen's Novels*, Blackwell, Oxford, 1981.

SOUTHAM, B. C.: *Jane Austen: The Critical Heritage*, Routledge and Kegan Paul, London, 1975.

SOUTHAM, B. C.: *Jane Austen: Sense and Sensibility, Pride and Prejudice and Mansfield Park*, (Casebook series) Macmillan, London, 1976.

TANNER, TONY: *Jane Austen*, Macmillan, London, 1986.

Background

ALLEN, WALTER: *The English Novel*, J. M. Dent, London, 1954.

The author of these notes

GEOFFREY PHILIP NASH was educated at New College, Oxford where he read English Language and Literature for his BA degree. He obtained his doctorate from London University on the work of Thomas Carlyle. He has taught English in both the United Kingdom and North Africa and has published several titles on nineteenth century themes.